SHE WAS IN and his lips were on hers as if he'd never let her go. Those hungry kisses were everything she'd dreamed about for so long—passion, need, and pure pleasure. The hands she felt caressing her were the skillful hands of an experienced lover, and she responded instinctively, deeply, giving herself up to the greatest joy she had ever known. . . .

Other SIGNET Books by Glenna Finley

LOVE FOR A ROGUE

by
Glenna Finley

Man may be formed of windlestraws,
but to make a rogue, you must have grist.

—SCHILLER

A SIGNET BOOK
NEW AMERICAN LIBRARY
TIMES MIRROR

SIGNET TRADEMARK REG. U.S. PAT. OFF. AND FOREIGN COUNTRIES
REGISTERED TRADEMARK—MARCA REGISTRADA
HECHO EN CHICAGO, U.S.A.

SIGNET, SIGNET CLASSICS, MENTOR, PLUME AND MERIDIAN BOOKS
are published by The New American Library, Inc.,
1301 Avenue of the Americas, New York, New York 10019

FIRST SIGNET PRINTING, AUGUST, 1976

1 2 3 4 5 6 7 8 9

PRINTED IN THE UNITED STATES OF AMERICA

Chapter One

Until that moment, the atmosphere at Canfield Camp in Oregon's Rogue River country could have served as the prototype for a peaceful summer morning in the wilderness.

The July sky was a bright blue scrubbed clean by the cotton clouds which still lingered over the rugged mountain tops of the Coast range. Branches of the towering Douglas firs and cedars on the riverbank hung heavy with dew as they rustled in the intermittent dawn breeze. The main camp building reared up between them, its gaunt wooden outline charitably softened by the early-morning light. Even the sagging porch which served to connect the old structure with a makeshift dormitory addition looked almost respectable.

Behind the camp, a rooster stalked back to his perch in the hen house after delivering a series of wake-up calls for the guests—annoyed that the premises remained deserted and undisturbed after his efforts.

He would have been pleased to learn that his crows were not all in vain; the shower in the lean-to hut by the sleeping rooms suddenly came to life, but even

1

that sound was camouflaged by the riffle of the river currents nearby.

This peaceful state of affairs lasted only a few more minutes—until Melanie Adams, the young woman under the shower, decided that she'd turn into an icicle if she lingered any longer and reached for the shower handle.

The next minute she was staring, wide-eyed, at the brass plumbing fixture which had come off in her hand. She frowned and started to shove it back in place when she discovered that the water cascading over her shoulders was rapidly changing from ice-cold to scalding hot.

Instinctively, she backed out of the way, pushing the shower curtain aside as she retreated. This brought her abruptly up against the frame door of the hut and caused her to scrape an elbow in the confusion.

By then, the hut was rapidly taking on the appearance of a Turkish bath, and Melanie decided evacuation was the only sensible course. Unfortunately, her towel was beyond reach at the back of the shower stall, thanks to the steaming deluge in-between. Even as she stood there, water overflowed the makeshift drain of the hut and started to edge toward her feet.

She snatched her thigh-length silk hoppi-coat from a nail on the back of the door and pulled it on. Then she yanked the door open and, as quickly, closed it behind her.

Although she was safe for the moment, she stared down at herself in dismay. Other than a pair of thongs, the short coat constituted her entire outfit and clung so tightly to every curve that the soft material could have been used for a blueprint of the female form. Such attire might be acceptable on the French Riviera, but Melanie knew very well that fashion modes on the Rogue River differed considerably. Obviously she had to get out of sight before anyone else at the camp turned out for an early shower.

She cinched the belt on her robe for security and was hurrying down the porch when the door of the room next to hers opened suddenly and she collided with a tall man in his early thirties wearing a pair of khaki shorts and a towel over his shoulders.

"Hey, take it easy . . ." His startled voice trailed off as he noted her disheveled but undeniably attractive state. "Room service?" he drawled hopefully, neglecting to remove his hand from her arm once she'd regained her balance.

"Don't be absurd!" Melanie snapped, pulling away with a tug that left no doubt as to her state of mind— despite her lack of covering.

He grinned and shrugged. "I'm glad. For a minute I thought I should have signed up for the American plan—but you'd never pass on my expense account." He pulled the towel from his shoulders, revealing a formidable expanse of tanned chest. "Are you through with the shower?"

She was thoroughly annoyed by then. "Yes. But you can't use it."

One dark eyebrow climbed, making his thin face look almost satanic with the skin stretched tight over his high cheekbones and stubborn jaw. His straight

3

dark brown hair showed glints of red in the sunlight and his impatient frown showed he had a temper to match it. "Okay . . . I'll bite. Why can't I use the shower?"

"Because it's broken, that's why." Melanie suddenly became aware of what she was clutching in the pocket of her hoppi-coat and produced the shower handle for him. "It came apart."

"What are you planning to do? Make a collection of these things?" he asked, taking it from her.

"That hadn't occurred to me," she replied just as calmly. "I tried to screw it back on but the water was too hot by then."

His air of nonchalance vanished. "Hot water? You mean all the hot water's going down the drain?"

"Well, yes . . . I guess so." As he wheeled suddenly and headed for the shower lean-to, she scurried behind him. "I thought you knew," she added helplessly as she saw him yank open the door and then slam it shut again when a cloud of steam billowed around his head. "What are you doing now?" she asked as he started around to the rear of the building.

"Looking for the cut-off. It must be around here somewhere. Ahh!" The last was said in a tone of satisfaction as he knelt and shoved aside a wooden cover on the ground. "Here it is. Now we're in business."

"I . . . I didn't know there was such a thing," she confessed as he tightened a round valve.

"If you plan to make a habit of this, you'd better find out," he said, standing upright and retrieving the shower handle from his back pocket. "Otherwise some-

4

body'll drop you in the middle of the river without your water-wings."

She ignored that and followed as he went around to the shower cubicle again. "Now—what are you going to do?"

He paused to look over his shoulder in undisguised amusement. "Look . . . what's with the questions? Are you a plumber's apprentice or conducting a government survey?"

Her chin went up stubbornly. "I caused this catastrophe. I have a right to know what's going on."

"All that's going on right now is the handle that you pulled off." He yanked open the door and impatiently waited for the steam to escape before he stepped inside to start repairs. "If I don't get this thing back in working condition before Chet wakes up, he'll throw us both out without asking questions."

"Is Chet the short man with glasses who snarls at people when they check in?"

"That's the one. Somebody said that he came upriver to get away from human beings but they made the mistake of following him."

"Only because they didn't know what they were getting into." She waved a hand at the ramshackle buildings. "This place will never make Fodor or the Michelin Guide."

"You're right—but most of us just use it for an overnight stop when we're tired of sleeping out. The beds aren't great but a roof keeps the rain off."

Melanie shivered and pulled her coat closer as she felt the breeze on her damp legs.

Her repairman must have had eyes in the back of his head. "You'd better go get some clothes on. All the excitement's over." He turned the shower handle slightly and frowned as he tested the temperature of the water. "Lukewarm. I'd better be next in line."

She drew back a step. "I'm sorry . . . I didn't mean to inconvenience anybody."

"That's okay. I didn't mean to sound so uncharitable, but I didn't get much sleep last night. Incidentally, my name's Brandt—Deke Brandt."

"I'm Melanie Adams." She paused a minute and then went on. "Haven't we met before?"

His glance jerked upward. "Your face isn't familiar . . ."

Her expression was amused. "I know. I just thought it was time you took a look at it."

His ears turned red. "Sorry. At least we'll recognize each other if we meet again."

"Don't count on it. I don't make a habit of appearing out in public like this." She paused before turning toward her cabin door, as he muttered something in reply. "I beg your pardon?"

He cleared his throat. "If you must know—I just said that 'it was a pity.' Almost worth shaving in lukewarm water." He sketched a brief salute. "Nice seeing you. Enjoy your stay."

She watched him disappear into the shower and close the door behind him.

Frowning slightly, she walked back to her room at the end of the porch and pushed open the door. She stood there and continued to scowl at the gloomy interior. There was no doubt that the decor at Canfield Camp went beyond the term "rustic accommodation." The mattress on the narrow brass bed sagged alarmingly. Next to it, a table made of rough lumber held a kerosene lantern which needed cleaning. The only closet facilities consisted of four nails pounded into the wall at the foot of the bed. A mirror and a bentwood chair completed the furnishing, and while the latter's design might have excited an antique collector, it left a lot to be desired for comfort.

"If I stay here for the two weeks I planned, they'll find me swinging from the rafters when it's time to leave," Melanie muttered. "One night and I'm already talking to myself."

Abruptly she turned and made her way back along the porch toward the shower. Deke Brandt almost walked into her when he emerged a minute later.

"What in the devil are you hanging around for?" he growled, finding her underfoot again.

"I wanted to talk to you."

"So we talk. Do you have something against clothes?"

"Of course not."

"Then put some on. You're starting to turn blue."

"This is important. I didn't want to miss you."

He grinned at her then. "Believe me, I'm not that hard to find."

"Well, you didn't say anything about staying for breakfast," she countered defensively.

"Probably because I didn't plan to." His eyebrows drew together in a puzzled line. "I can . . . if it's necessary. Look—go in and get dressed while I shave.

Afterwards, trot over to the main building and tell Chet to put another cup of coffee on." At her relieved look, he became more brusque. "And if you have some slacks, put them on. Men around here aren't used to an outfit like the one you're wearing."

Once again, Melanie found herself staring at his disappearing back, but this time she smiled with satisfaction and adjourned to her room.

When she emerged ten minutes later, she was pretty sure Deke would approve of her nylon windbreaker and khaki slacks. Even the flyspecked mirror on her wall confirmed that the chino cloth bush pants "accentuated the positive" of her trim figure. So did her pale blond hair which she'd brushed in a soft wave over her ears. A pair of hazel eyes showed that she was able to view life with humor and discernment, and her lips were invitingly curved. If her rounded chin looked more stern than usual that morning, it was because she found her current predicament not entirely to her liking.

Her nose twitched as she hesitated on the steps of the porch. The air was tangy but smoky, too . . . that meant someone was stirring in the main building. With luck, the coffee pot might be functioning as well as the cook stove.

Melanie let her glance go once more toward Deke's closed door before she walked on to the older wing. It wouldn't do to put all her hopes on an unknown quality, she told herself. Especially when that unknown quality had appeared remarkably immune to feminine wiles. Any appeal she made in the future would have to be from another approach.

She was sitting disconsolately at a rough picnic table outside the kitchen when Deke found her a little later. He viewed her plate of untouched hotcakes and raised his eyebrows. "Now you can understand why I'd decided to skip breakfast," he drawled. "Chet doesn't count on repeat business from his guests."

"I wasn't even given a choice. He pushed this plate at me and left without a word."

"Knew there wasn't any use hanging around." Deke took a swallow from the mug he was holding. "At least the coffee's drinkable."

"Oh, I don't care about breakfast," she assured him in a rush. "But I'm supposed to stay here for two weeks."

He whistled softly. "How did you ever get wangled into that?"

She tried to explain. "Look—I work in Washington, D. C. When my boss gave me two weeks off in the middle of the summer, I certainly didn't argue. He even suggested this Rogue River country—said that I needed to breathe some air that I couldn't see. He was out here fishing once and never forgot it."

"If he stayed here at Canfield, I'm not surprised."

"He didn't," Melanie explained patiently. "This place was the only lodge on the river that my travel agent could find listed. And just wait until the next time I see her."

"You'd better head down to Gold Beach. That's a town on the ocean with plenty of places to stay."

"But I don't *want* to stay on the ocean," she said, shoving aside her coffee mug. "I told everybody that I was coming out to stay in the Rogue wilderness area. If I'd wanted an ocean resort, I could have gone to New Jersey."

"There is a difference . . ."

"New Jersey has some very nice beach resorts," she told him with asperity.

"I was merely pointing out that we're talking about two different oceans," he said calmly. "Atlantic City doesn't have to get its dander up."

She shook her head despairingly. "I'm sorry. I'm making an awful hash of it. I'd like to find another place on the Rogue—I hoped you could suggest one."

"You mean around here?" He frowned as she nodded. "I'm afraid you're out of luck. How do you think Chet gets his unsuspecting lodgers? Even the rafters traveling the river complain about the camp's accommodations."

"Would you mind sitting down while we talk?" She smiled as she gestured toward the other side of the table. "I'd hate to get a crick in my neck, too. It's the only place that doesn't ache after a night on that mattress."

Deke looked at her more carefully, but he slid onto the bench opposite. "One night shouldn't throw you."

"Evidently not all of us have your rugged constitution," she snapped back.

"Evidently." He was trying hard to keep a straight face and not doing too well. "What do you do in Washington, D.C.?"

"A kind of research."

"You can be more specific than that."

"Well, lately I've been working on surveys and questionnaires for various bureaus," she said after a little hesitation. "Let me know if you need a job. You'd be good at the questionnaires."

"You were the one who started all this," he pointed out with masculine logic. "I'm entitled to a few answers." He took another sip of coffee. "Are you planning a government survey around here?"

"Certainly not. I just earned some time off because my boss has a new project lined up later in the summer."

"So in the meantime, you're getting a vacation on the Oregon coast."

"That has all the hallmarks of a nasty crack. If you *must* know, my doctor suggested I take a vacation. I'd put in a lot of overtime to make the deadline on our last survey."

He shifted slightly on the bench to take advantage of a patch of shade. "Sounds like quite a project. What was it on?"

"The physical fitness of American adults." Her chin went up defiantly. "You needn't laugh like that."

"Sorry. I just happened to have a normal ingrained taxpayer's resentment toward government surveys. You'll feel better after a day or so in Gold Beach . . . the ocean's good for putting problems in the right perspective. Get Chet to take you into town when he drives in for provisions today." He was still smiling as he stood up, "I'm sorry to leave but I'm late for an appointment now. Maybe I'll see you in town. Sometimes I get down at the weekend."

She spoke up as he started to move away. "You mean you're going to stay here until then?"

He swung round to face her, scowling slightly. "No . . . I'm leaving now. I make my base upriver." At her puzzled expression, he went on. "I'm a field geologist. My job is checking into the ore deposits in this area."

"Then you camp out?"

"No . . . not exactly," he replied with some evasiveness. "There's a place called Tukwila Lodge upriver that I use for a headquarters."

Her head came up alertly. "Another camp like this one?"

"Hardly. A man would starve to death here before the month was out. Tukwila is smaller and has all the amenities, but I'm afraid it's booked for the summer. You'll like the places down at the ocean though." He looked at his watch. "Damn! I'll never make it over the ridge by noon if I don't get a move on." His glance raked her discouraged profile. "I'll definitely make it a point to get down to the beach this weekend. What about dinner on Saturday?"

"How will you know where to find me?"

He grinned. "After looking for ore deposits around here, finding you in Gold Beach is no trouble. I'll see you then." He gave her a brief salute and disappeared down the stairs at the end of the porch.

It was a half hour later before Melanie managed to corner the manager of the camp as he sauntered toward the dusty van used for transporting supplies and guests into town.

The short, stocky man pulled to a stop at her approach. His eyes narrowed behind the thick glasses that he wore halfway down his nose. "Was there something else you wanted, lady?" Then before she could answer, "Lunch isn't served till I get back from town and that'll be quite a spell."

"I'm afraid I won't be here for it, after all. That's what I wanted to tell you. I've changed my plans but naturally I don't expect any refund."

His face, which had been growing more stricken all the time, resumed its normal impassivity. As the full import registered, he rubbed a thumb along his bristly chin. "That means you won't be eatin' meals here."

She beamed back at him, equally pleased for the same reason. "That's right. All you have to do is tell me how to get to Tukwila Lodge and I'll be on my way."

His thumb stopped abruptly. "Tukwila? You mean you're staying there?"

"I planned to. Why?" She kept her voice casual.

"Didn't think Obie was takin' any overnighters. Never known him to before. I heard just the other day that he was havin' a hell of a time finding any help this summer. Obie Roberts," he went on impatiently as she stared blankly at him, "the guy who takes care of the lodge."

"Oh, yes. Mr. Roberts. I'd forgotten his name," Melanie said, keeping her fingers crossed.

"Well, if you're fixin' to work for Obadiah, you'd

better remember it. He's in a bad mood about having to hire more help this season. Tukwila hasn't had skirts around, regular-like, for quite a spell."

"That's unusual, isn't it?"

"Don't see why. The mining people staying there don't look for fun and games at the lodge . . . not when there's plenty of excitement at the beach resorts. You'll find it pretty dull up there, but I suppose a job's a job these days."

Melanie nodded thoughtfully. "I'm all packed and it'll only take a minute to get my gear. If you won't mind giving me a ride—"

He interrupted before she'd taken more than a step or two. "You must be confused, lady. I couldn't take you to Tukwila if I wanted to." His fat stomach surged with laughter. "Not unless I grew pontoons. That lodge's upriver and my van can't handle the track. The best way is for you to hitch a ride on the mail boat."

The flicker of alarm which made itself felt in Melanie's midsection subsided again. "What time does the mail boat come by?"

"Round about eleven. Be down on the dock so you can flag him down if you have to . . . though he's usually got something to deliver. We've been getting lots of response on our ads in the travel sections back East."

"I can imagine." It went without saying that only unsuspecting souls a continent away would apply. Obviously none of the local gentry touched Canfield Camp except in sheer necessity and then left as soon as possible. She said instead, "Thanks for everything. I'll be down on the dock in plenty of time."

"Okay, lady." Chet must have felt a prepaid guest who obligingly checked out on the first day of her stay deserved a little more. "Good luck up at Tukwila . . . with the job, I mean. Tell Obadiah to call if you need a reference."

Melanie hid a smile. "I will."

The man nodded and opened the van door. A minute later, he'd backed out of the drive and was accelerating down the dusty road, paying scant attention to the potholes dotting its surface.

By the time eleven o'clock rolled around, the temperature on the riverbank had risen fully thirty degrees. Melanie had long since shed her jacket, draping it over her bags on the wooden dock, before she perched on a flat rock nearby. In front of her, the powerful river surged swiftly around Canfield bend, its emerald water matching the evergreen foliage on its steep banks.

She heard an engine whine heralding the arrival of the mail boat long before the craft was visible. When it finally spurted into view around the promontory, it was a trim-looking aluminum inboard about twenty-five feet long with a relaxed boatman in his late twenties handling the stern controls. He wheeled the craft in toward her with professional ease; gunning the engine to bring the hull around, then cutting the power and letting it side-slip until the craft rested neatly in the water alongside the dock.

Melanie's eyes gleamed with appreciation. "Were

you just lucky or could you do it again?" she asked the man as he stood to toss her the bow line.

He grinned amiably and made fast at the stern before coming over beside her. "I can do it with my eyes closed, but it helps if there's a pretty girl waiting on the dock. I'm partial to an admiring audience." Although he was just about medium height, his frame looked powerful in shorts and a casual T-shirt. His blond hair was trimmed but worn fairly long around a pleasant, ordinary face. The ease with which he moved around the boat showed that he'd garnered most of his bronzed skin on the river run.

Melanie became aware suddenly that he was surveying her just as intently.

"You don't have enough sunburn for a rafter and you're too clean to have been hiking," he announced. "If you're thinking of thumbing a ride, I'll have to remind you that this is an official U.S. mail boat . . ."

She looked appropriately impressed. "But you do take freight?"

"Absolutely." He was quick on the uptake. "Live freight or oversized packages. What's your destination?"

"Tukwila Lodge."

"Tukwila?" His unassuming features went blank suddenly. "What are you going to do there?"

"Mr. Brandt told me about it," she replied evasively. "Earlier this morning."

"And he told you to hitch a ride?" There was skepticism in the boatman's tone. "That doesn't sound like Deke. Unless he's changed his ways and invited you for some forbidden fruits." He must have sensed her withdrawal because he grinned suddenly and said, "Sorry, I should have introduced myself . . . I'm Les Roberts. My dad manages Tukwila. That's why all the questions. I've never known Deke to mix business and pleasure during the summer season before."

"I'm Melanie Adams." She hesitated before saying more, wondering why there was no mention of transient guests at Tukwila Lodge. Evidently that possibility was out—and there was no point in pretending a sudden friendship with Deke Brandt. That would be nipped in the bud as soon as he encountered her again. Suddenly the words of the Canfield Camp manager came to her aid. "I heard your father was hiring some temporary help and I'm . . . between jobs . . . at the moment." Just then she couldn't have said why she was so persistent or why she was being devious with Les Roberts. Perhaps it was his obvious reluctance to take her to Tukwila . . . the same reluctance that Deke Brandt had exhibited earlier that morning.

Les's expression smoothed at her announcement. "I'm afraid you're too late. Our new help's practically hired."

"Practically?"

"Well, as good as. She's an old friend of ours and has agreed to fill in for the rest of the season. I'm going to tell Dad when I deliver the mail." He frowned as he saw the disappointment on her face. "You say you talked to Deke?"

Melanie considered his words and decided she

could safely agree with that. "Yes, this morning. But he didn't promise anything," she added truthfully.

"Maybe you'd better talk to Dad, anyhow," Les said after a moment's pause. "Deke can be stiff-necked at times. Who knows—you might sue us for not being an equal opportunity employer."

She bestowed an answering smile. "Well, there's always that chance."

"And there's plenty to do up at the lodge. The budget could run to another job if you play your cards right." Les spoke easily as he went over to pick up her baggage and transferred it to the boat. "Ready to go?" At her nod, he held out a strong hand and helped her into the boat, indicating a seat just in front of his control panel. "Sit down there. You'll have to put on a life jacket, too—there's one under the seat." At her blank look, he went on to explain. "Regulations for this part of the river. Some of the riffles are a little hairy from here on up to Tukwila and the Coast Guard objects if I lose any 'packages' overboard. You have to be especially careful if you're the only cargo."

"Why is that?"

His grin widened. "I'm not allowed to stop if there's only one body overboard. Remember to always take a friend with you."

Melanie shook her head sadly. "I certainly walked into that one." She watched him deftly release the bow and stern lines as the current started to move the boat away from the dock. Les gunned the engines into life and rested a hip against his chair by the boat's control panel as he made for the center of the river and then upstream.

Melanie felt the wind whip her face and tightened her grip on the side of the boat as their speed increased. After a few moments she took a thrilled breath and raised her voice over the throaty roar of the engines, "How fast are we going now?"

It was evident that Les caught the excitement in her words because he winked and said proudly, "About twenty to twenty-five miles per hour. I can add another five to it when we're going downstream with the current."

Melanie peered over the side and looked up again with a perplexed expression. "But it's so shallow . . . it can't be more than a foot deep. Why don't we run aground?"

Les wheeled the craft toward two markers in the swift-moving water. "Because I'm staying in the middle of the channel. As long as we have six to eight inches of water under us, we're in business. It's all done with pumps instead of the regular type of outboard," he explained, raising his voice over the noise. "These jet river boats don't have a rudder—all the steering is done by directing the spray of water. There's fantastic control." He nodded toward some white water ahead of them. "And there has to be here on the Rogue. Hang on—this stretch will bounce you around."

Melanie gasped and clutched the side of the aluminum boat as he accelerated and cut through the center of the turbulent rapids. The craft catapulted through the rough, tumbling waters even as Melanie caught sight of a protruding rock only two feet from their bow. Her eyes widened, but before she could shout a warning, Les had gunned his throttle again and the craft was turning to meet another dangerous stretch. Then, the bottom of the boat slapped down hard on the surface like a bronc trying to unseat its rider, and Melanie crouched low to stay aboard.

"Are you okay?" Les called down to her.

She waited until they were through the final white water before raising her head. "Marvelous! I didn't know anything could be such fun. Will there be more like that?"

"Only one more set that's worth noticing before Tukwila. That's where 'Wake Up Murphy' Creek hits the main stream. It's a real rollercoaster. Then the river settles down and behaves itself."

Melanie nodded and settled back. Her entranced gaze wandered over the heavily forested banks where an occasional outcropping of granite provided a rugged primeval touch to the wooded background. Les seemed to appreciate her awe and pointed out other items of interest like the osprey nest at the top of a fir snag.

"There are dozens of them on the riverbanks," he informed her. "You'd never guess that nest measures six feet across, would you?"

She shook her head in wonderment. "Until now, I thought an osprey was just something in crossword puzzles. You know, a six-letter word for fish hawk."

"I prefer mine in the flesh. That's Mama on the top limb close to the nest." He slowed his speed so she could see where he was pointing. "Probably looking for something for lunch. Ospreys catch and kill their prey—won't eat anything unless it's already dead."

"Ugh!" Melanie wrinkled her nose with distaste. "Sounds too much like a vulture for me. You must have lived around here most of your life to be such an expert on things."

His lips twisted. "My dad wouldn't agree with you. According to him, nobody under fifty knows anything or has his head screwed on right these days. That's why I'm back working on the river this summer. I have to earn money to finish graduate school. Dad thinks any more 'book-learning' "—Les drawled the word out—"is a waste of time. If I want it, I have to pay for it."

"You don't look old enough for graduate school."

"You should talk." Les's good-natured grin reappeared. "I've got a year or two on you, I'll bet. How old *are* you . . . twenty-one, twenty-two?"

"Thanks for the kind words. I'm almost twenty-five."

"Then we're kindred souls. Tell me the truth, Melanie." His sharp glance rested on her for a moment. "What are you doing up here? You don't look like the kind of woman to be on the dock at Canfield."

"I know. Too clean and not enough sunburn." She reached up to tie a scarf over her head as the breeze whipped her hair. "That last part doesn't apply any longer. My nose is peeling already."

"Don't change the subject," he reproved lazily.

"There's not much to tell. I'd heard about the Rogue wilderness area and I had some time off . . ." Belatedly she remembered that she was supposed to be looking for a job and went on hurriedly. "Time off that I didn't expect."

"Fired, huh?" He didn't wait for her answer. "Well, don't get your hopes up—anything at the lodge is strictly temporary. Just for the summer. Once our rainy season sets in, we close up shop. The river becomes too much to handle."

"You mean people like Mr. Brandt move on." Melanie asked carefully.

"Deke? Sure. He'd probably like to stay longer but he's a busy man. Somebody who knows where he's going, as Dad'll tell you. Deke's been held up to me as the 'Great White Hope' ever since I can remember."

"Oh? He didn't go out of his way to impress me." As Melanie thought back on it, Deke Brandt's impatience to be on his way was the only part of their conversation that stood out. Even his arrangement for a dinner date at the beach had been an obvious afterthought.

"Deke's not one for chatting up females . . . even ones as pretty as you. Not during the summer months. He doesn't talk about what he does the rest of the time and I don't think it would be good policy to ask." Les ran a finger graphically across his jugular vein. "Mr. Brandt has a way of telling people off in 'ten not-very-polite words or less' if he gets annoyed. Not that it happens often—but when it does, you remember it."

"Thanks for warning me. I'll try to stay out of his way."

"First things first," he corrected. "We haven't even got you on the premises yet. My dad can be pretty stubborn about hiring women help although he's partial to blondes. My mother had hair the color of yours." For an instant, Les's voice had a different quality, then it went back to its normal tones. "Anyway, we'll see. If you strike out, I'll take you back down to the beach this afternoon."

"Thanks, I hope it won't be necessary." She could see the river narrowing again and the current moving faster as it swept past the rocky crags of the bend ahead. "Is this the part you were telling me about?"

"Yep. Cobra Rock is the one we go by on the left. It's reached out and snagged plenty of boats in its time. Don't worry, these jets lower the risks—besides, it's getting hot enough to enjoy a swim." His grin was a white slash across his tanned face.

"I've already had one shower today," she called back to him over the sound of the turbulent white water ahead.

"Then I'll watch where I'm going. Hang on . . . here we go!" Just a few minutes after they'd passed through that exhilarating stretch, Les shot the boat around a wide bend of the Rogue and gestured ahead of them. "There you are! Tukwila Lodge . . . right on schedule."

"But . . . but it's beautiful! I didn't expect anything like that!" was all Melanie could say as she stared at the rambling two-story structure high on the riverbank among the trees. The exterior of the lodge was a mixture of stone and cedar, the latter a lovely silver color brought about by a gradual weathering through the seasons. Deep eaves protected the wide windows of the main wing which overlooked the river and fronted onto an extensive stone deck. This was edged by a line of flowerbeds and boxes bursting with colorful blossoms. On a lower level, a modern rectangular swimming pool was surrounded by redwood lounges cushioned in bright yellow and green canvas. A companion wing to the right of the main structure was connected by a contemporary breezeway. Each window of the smaller wing had its own cedar balcony to provide an even closer glimpse of the spectacular scenery.

Melanie gave Les a reproachful glance as he cut the speed of the engine and let the boat glide the final few feet up to a short dock. "No *wonder* everyone was keeping so quiet about this place! If I owned anything like it, I'd go around like a clam, too."

"You mean that's what Deke did?"

"Uh-huh." She wasn't paying close attention as her fascinated gaze was still on the building above the dock. "He just said something about making this his base of operations. And all the time he was trying to talk me into staying on the beach."

"He probably thought there'd be more jobs down there." Les jumped lightly onto the dock to secure the lines and held out a hand to help her. "He's right about that. And if you were working down there, it would be easier all around. Shall we take your bags up or should we wait until you've landed a job?"

"Let's take them up." After glimpsing Tukwila, Melanie was determined to spend part of her vacation there one way or another. "Can't I carry something?"

Her gaze went back to the boat. "What about that mail on the seat? Does it go here?"

He nodded after hoisting her bags. "Sure—bring it along. It'll save me a trip. There are some other supplies but they can wait."

"Whatever you say." She leaned over to stack the bundle of mail and started to wrap a newspaper around it. "I haven't seen one of these for a couple of days," she said, scanning the headlines as she folded it. "Apparently there's nothing new in the world—except for a drowning up the coast and a bank robbery." Her lips pursed in a silent whistle. "They got away with a hundred thousand dollars—somebody plays in the major leagues around here."

"You don't have to bring that thing along."

"It's no trouble." She slipped it under her arm and followed him along the path which twisted up from the dock toward the swimming pool, eventually changing to neat stone steps leading on to the deck. "I'm surprised to see a pool here. I heard at the camp last night that most people swim in the river."

"You can do that, too, if you want to. There's even a rock on the bank around the bend that you can use for a diving board. Most of the visiting kids like that best."

She paused in surprise. "Are there children staying at Tukwila?"

"Not right now. I think there are some families coming in later . . . a get-together of mining company employees." He sounded slightly out-of-breath as they reached the pool level. "Go on up," he said, nodding

25

toward the steps. "If I know Dad, he's out fussing in the garden someplace."

That time, Les was wrong in his reckoning. Obie Roberts wasn't out on the deck inspecting the planters filled with flowers, nor was he on the far side of the lodge where neat rows of plants provided a cutting garden. Even the small greenhouse just beyond stood empty in the bright sunshine. It wasn't until they went through the magnificently carved wooden door of the lodge itself that they found the manager.

Even at first glimpse, Melanie could see the likeness between the two Roberts men. The elder had a lion-like mane of gray hair instead of Les's towhead shade but he boasted the same wide forehead and deep-set eyes in a deeply tanned skin. Although wrinkles around his features gave him a weatherbeaten appearance, he was still a formidable figure in khaki pants and short-sleeved shirt as he straightened by the fireplace hearth to stare at them.

"Dad . . . I'd like you to meet Melanie Adams. She hitched a ride with me up from Canfield."

"How d'you do, Miss Adams. It's a pleasure to meet you." The manager came forward to shake hands with her—his courtly manner from another era like stovepipe hats or parasols in the park.

Melanie smiled at him. "I'm glad to meet you, Mr. Roberts."

" 'Obie' does fine up here," he interrupted in an accent that made him sound more like a transplanted New Englander than anything else. "Nobody says Mr. Roberts."

"And he doesn't encourage Obadiah—so you'd better forget that, too," Les put in slyly. "It's too much of a mouthful to be handy. Isn't that right, Dad?"

One thick gray eyebrow rose to censure him. "Seems to me you're in no position to talk."

"Too right." The younger man turned back to Melanie and admitted, "He's got me. Les is the handle for Lester Beauregard—my mother's choice—" He broke off as he saw her lips twitch and grinned in response. "Now you've heard about the skeleton in our family closet."

"I can't think why she'd care much about it, since she's just visiting. Go on and show her around, Les, while I heat up the coffee pot," Obie said.

"Yeah . . . sure." Les shifted uneasily. "The only thing is . . . Melanie wanted to talk to you. But I guess it can wait a while."

"At least until we have coffee," Melanie put in with haste, unsure of the best way to approach Les's father. Now that she was face-to-face with Obadiah Roberts, the chances of getting a temporary job seemed more remote than ever.

"Well, whatever you say." The manager scratched the back of his neck and moved toward the dining room archway. "I'll take care of the coffee. Les, did you talk to Martha about filling in?"

"Yeah . . ." The younger man trailed behind him, after making a hasty gesture to reassure Melanie before he left the room. "She'll be up in a couple days. It'll take that long for her sister to come from Portland to stay in her house down at the beach."

"Two days!" Obie's querulous voice was still audible even as the swinging door to the kitchen closed behind them. "I could use her sooner. Miss Hendricks is due anytime . . ."

Who in the dickens was Miss Hendricks, Melanie wondered. For an all-masculine habitat, Tukwila would soon have a full quiver of females. Now, if only she could manage still another feminine addition to the roster, everything would be marvelous.

She moved aimlessly over to the floor-to-ceiling windows which covered the front of the sitting room on either side of the big native stone fireplace. The room was furnished in essentially masculine fashion with deep upholstered chairs and divans in rust and cinnamon atop a beige rug. Its beige tone was repeated in wide draw curtains and in the scattered oak end tables. Beyond the fireplace, a small leather bar filled the far corner. Melanie's attention focused on the big tropical fish tank beside it, and she moved over to study it with real interest. There was a beautiful setting of organ pipe and branch coral on a bed of gleaming white marble chips to provide a background for the exotic saltwater specimens. At the front of the tank, an amusing yellow-green cowfish followed her finger in hopes of an extra meal.

When Melanie heard movement in the kitchen, she reluctantly turned away and was staring onto the deck by the time the men came in. Obie was carrying a wooden tray with cups on it and Les, staring sullenly at his father's back, held a porcelain coffee pot in one hand. Melanie noted how he avoided looking her way and felt a pang of apprehension.

"Put down your things and find a chair, Melanie." Obie sounded heartier than before. "I imagine you could use some coffee."

Attuned to all nuances, she decided it was the tone of a polite man unsure of how to administer a polite but firm refusal. But then, his words penetrated and she looked down in some surprise to find that she was still carrying the mail and newspaper she'd collected from the boat. "Oh, I'm sorry, these are yours." She moved over to hand them to him as he deposited the coffee things on the nearest end table. "I was so fascinated by your marine aquarium that I forgot to deliver them. You have some beautiful fish."

Obie took the mail automatically and started to sort idly through it. "Are you interested in tropicals?"

"I have a small set-up at home," Melanie admitted. "It was hard getting someone to look after it when I came out here. My fish are partial to live food like brine shrimp—"

"I know just what you mean," Obie interrupted, glancing up in surprise. "There's a tomato clown in that tank who sulks if he doesn't get scallops once a day. That means I've got to be around and hand-feed him. Folks don't realize—"

"Let me pour the coffee before it gets cold," Les said, cutting him off. He winked at Melanie. "You can talk fish another time."

Obie subsided obediently. "I'd sure like to." He looked at her and frowned as if trying to reach a decision. "Talk fish, I mean. It would be nice to have a little extra help with them. Lester mentioned you wanted a job, Melanie . . . when we were out in the kitchen. I told him I didn't know how we could arrange it. Martha . . . a lady from the beach," he added carefully, "is coming up to cook for us for the rest of the season. She's experienced and needs the money. Of course, we take care of our own quarters and I manage the gardens," he waved a hand toward the deck.

"I understand." This time it was Melanie who interrupted gently. "I meant to compliment you on your flowers. The boxes of marigolds and lobelia are perfectly gorgeous. That two-tone variety is the one called 'Paprika', isn't it?"

"Yes, but there's another marigold called 'Lulu' out under the kitchen window that I'm partial to. I've used dwarf marguerites in the planters there—" He broke off as an idea suddenly occurred to him. "Say—are you fussy about what kind of a job you have?"

Melanie kept her voice level with an effort. "Not if it lets me stay at this wonderful place a while. And I promise not to make off with the silverware."

He waved that aside. "Well, I certainly could use some help outside. Deke told me I was a fool to plant so much garden this spring but I guess it's a habit." His hooded appraisal wandered over her tense figure. "If I wanted to hire some temporary help, I don't imagine there'd be any problems. Mind you, I expect hard work . . . no slacking off because you're female." He raised his hand when she would have protested. "I know all about women's rights—Les's girl friends have set me straight on that." His gray-blue eyes flickered with amusement. "At least, they think they have."

Melanie took a deep breath and let it out slowly. "You'll get your money's worth," she promised sincerely. "Where would you like me to start?"

"Everything growing round the patio needs water and fertilizing," he said, considering. "This dry weather's playing hob with my plants."

"I'll get right to it."

"Well, finish your coffee first and then Les'll show you to a room. You can pretty much take your pick in the guest wing." Obie sank back against the lounge cushion and started to sort through the mail she'd brought. "Later on, we'll figure out about supper. If we're going to have company . . ." His voice came to an abrupt stop and his hands clutched the printed matter in his lap as the color drained from his face. Both Les and Melanie could see how he labored over his next breath.

"Dad! What's the matter?" The younger man got to his feet anxiously.

"What in the hell d'you suppose?" Obie's voice lashed out querulously.

"It's his heart." Les threw the quick comment over his shoulder as Melanie came uncertainly to his side. "He has a bottle of blue pills over the sink in the kitchen. Bring it and some water. And hurry!"

She was halfway there when she heard Obie start to mutter painfully. "How much can a man take? I just don't give a damn any more—"

Les cut into his wanderings. "Simmer down. There'll

be plenty of time for talking later. Don't say any more now." Then Melanie was through the swinging door of the kitchen and looking for the bottle she'd been sent to get.

Her surroundings of stainless steel and gleaming porcelain registered only dully as did the cheerful view over a patch of lawn and the vegetable garden beyond. Her attention was riveted on snatching up Obie's medicine and, after that, a quick search of the walnut kitchen cabinets for a glass. Then she was hurrying back into the living room with her hands full.

Obie was still upright on the couch, but his head was switching back and forth on the cushion as if he were suffering considerable pain.

"Here are the pills." Melanie shoved the plastic bottle into Les's outstretched hand as he hovered beside his father. She watched Les shake out two pills in his palm and say, with unwonted gentleness, "Here, Dad . . . open your mouth," and had the glass of water ready when he reached for it.

Obie swallowed with an effort and then flopped back against the cushion again as if the minuscule effort had drained him.

"Is there a doctor I can call?" Melanie asked in a low voice.

The query brought a flicker of amusement to Les's features. "It isn't that easy . . . there's no phone up here. The fastest way to get help is by boat or helicopter, but I'm hoping it won't be necessary. The pills should do the trick. Isn't that right, Dad?"

Obie chose to ignore the entreaty in his son's voice.

When he looked up, his reply was directed at Melanie. "No need to get in a panic, young lady. I'm not about to check out yet." His ironic glance moved on to Les. "Help me to my room—then you get back here and show Melanie where she'll sleep. I'll only need an hour or so's rest."

From the gray color of his face, Melanie privately thought his forecast seemed more optimistic than realistic, and she decided to have words with Les about it as soon as she could. Aloud she said soothingly, "Don't worry about things, Mr. Roberts—everything will work out fine."

"Ummm." From his monosyllabic response, it was hard to tell whether Obie was unconvinced or simply didn't care. He allowed Les to help him up and leaned heavily on him as they went slowly from the room, disappearing through a door next to the dining room.

It wasn't long before Les returned alone, a grim look on his face.

"He's not worse, is he?" Melanie asked quickly.

"Not that I could see." His voice was brusque as he reached for her luggage. "If the stubborn old fool will just take things easy . . ."

"He certainly shouldn't be planning any work today."

"We won't have to argue about that. The pills will knock him out for a couple of hours and then some." He led the way across the breezeway and up a flight of carpeted stairs in the guest wing, stopping in front of a door halfway down the hall. "Open it, will you?"

"Of course." She twisted the knob and then stepped

back to let him enter the room first. As he put her cases on two racks near the door, she walked across the spacious bedroom to feast on the view through a sliding glass balcony door. The wide twisting river framed by the rugged forested hills provided a setting so tranquil and delightful that it was an effort for Melanie to turn her back on it. She made a gesture of surrender to Les and went out to lean against the balcony railing. "How," she inquired, "does a woman go about getting a permanent job here?"

"You wouldn't ask if you knew how hard it rains in the wintertime."

"I have a feeling that's enemy propaganda." She leaned over the wooden balcony railing. "There must be four shades of green on that mountain peak over there alone."

He laughed at her enthusiasm. "How do you think all that greenery comes about? They don't call Oregon football teams the Webfoots for nothing."

"I refuse to be discouraged." She left the balcony reluctantly and came back in to admire the bedroom furnishings. Her glance noted the thick carpet and the restful neutral grasscloth on the wall behind the teak bed and bureau. An open door beyond revealed a gleaming tiled bath. "This is so elegant—are you sure that I'm supposed to be here? Don't forget that I'm a working stiff now."

He grinned and scratched his jaw, looking more like the relaxed young man she'd known on the trip up-river. "Who deserves it more? Don't worry, nobody's stuffed in the garret around here."

"Then I'm going to change in about five minutes flat and get to work. Remind me to stay off the balcony—that scenery's so beautiful that I could spend hours there and I don't want to take a chance of getting fired before I can enjoy all this." She followed him as he started toward the hall. "I almost forgot to ask . . . where should I start?"

"Damned if I know. Outside's as good a place as any, I guess."

"But what about your father? Shouldn't I stay within call, or will you handle that?"

Les frowned. "He's perfectly okay now. There's no need to do anything but look in every half hour or so and see if he wants anything. I have to make a delivery upriver but I'll be back before long." At her stricken expression, he added, "There's no need for you to worry. I'll check on him last thing before I go."

"Well, if you say so . . ."

"I do." He paused in the middle of the corridor. "Go pull up some weeds, but *don't* pull up any of his prize seedlings or he'll have a stroke plus his heart trouble. If you want anything to eat, just raid the refrigerator. I'll get a sandwich when I come back." With a casual wave he was gone, his steps almost indiscernible on the thickly carpeted stairs.

Melanie went back in the bedroom and closed the door behind her. As she rummaged for an old pair of shorts that wouldn't show grass stains or dirt, she was giving thanks that Obie had offered her a job before he'd been stricken. Now she could work with a clear conscience, she told herself as she shucked off her slacks and hung them in the closet. Not having to worry about his plants and fish might even help the manager's recovery. She'd have to ask Les later if she should cook the meals as well. An extra hand would probably be welcome if other guests were arriving.

She combed her hair and was on her way to the door when she suddenly remembered the unknown Miss Hendricks that Obie had mentioned. That meant she should ask if a guest room needed preparing. Automatically her thoughts moved on to Deke Brandt. From the way he'd spoken, he must already have a room at the lodge. Another thing to be checked with the Roberts men.

As she hurried down the stairs and back toward the main building, her lips were curved in pure enjoyment. It would be fun to see the expression on Deke's features when they finally came face to face again! He certainly wouldn't expect to find her already employed at the lodge. Melanie's mischievous expression deepened. Maybe her maneuver would make Mr. Brandt think twice about saying Tukwila was fully booked when the next traveler asked.

She decided against bothering with lunch until later, and made her way to the greenhouse just beyond the cutting bed. She was inside sniffing the impressive collection of imperial lilies and admiring some pots of bougainvillea when she heard the departure noise of Les's mail boat.

"Better get to work," she told herself sternly. It would be nice to report some tangible progress when he returned.

Accordingly, she checked the moisture in the greenhouse and then the big square planter boxes full of white petunias on the deck. She set soakers in the beds and watered the patio boxes by hand, afterward mixing fertilizer in a sprinkling can to apply it as a top dressing on the damp soil. When she'd finished on the deck, she moved down the steps to take care of the planter boxes there.

She wiped the perspiration from her forehead after connecting a hose for the preliminary watering and allowed herself a wistful glance at the swimming pool. It would be wonderful to cool off in its clear depths, she thought, and then gave herself a mental prod. She was here as a paid employee—not as a paying guest. "Back to the salt mines," she told herself sternly and turned on the hose. When she heard voices emerging above her on the deck, she had just finished watering a planter of marigolds by the deep end of the pool.

"Well, I didn't expect this place to be deserted," came a clear feminine tone. "Deke, you'll have to speak to Obie . . . he's supposed to be on duty and he's probably buried himself in the garden again."

Then Deke Brandt's deep voice said, considerably closer, "Frankly, I'd rather bury myself in the pool. It must be close to a hundred today . . . let's check the thermometer."

"Where is it?" his companion wanted to know.

"Over here in the corner."

Melanie crouched low, keeping close to the marigolds as she turned off the water. With any luck, she could stay out of sight until the two had gone back to the lodge. Then she could dash to her room and put on something decent before explaining her presence.

Above her, Deke's voice sounded again. "Ninety-five. No wonder it was hot in the truck. When I trade it in on a new model, I'm going to weaken and get air-conditioning. Usually you don't need it around here."

"I'll alert the financial department to watch your expense account," his companion said with amusement. "Let's go down and test the temperature in the pool. I hope Obie checked that before he disappeared."

"Jessica—you're terrific! I never knew anybody with such a practical approach." Deke appeared at the head of the stairs, his attention still on the woman behind him.

His appearance made Melanie realize the futility of trying to remain hidden. She straightened awkwardly from her crouched position by the planter box and took an instinctive step backward. Unfortunately, her foot came into contact with the hose coiled on the concrete behind her. She teetered, trying to regain her balance, and succeeded in tangling her other foot as well, finally pitching backward onto the mish-mash of hose. Even that wasn't catastrophic, as she wasn't injured and she had avoided the indignity of going head-first into the pool.

But as she struggled hastily to pull herself up, her arm came into contact with the sprinkling can and managed to upset its entire two gallons of fishy-smelling plant fertilizer squarely onto her lap.

Deke Brandt took the short steps to the pool level in one leap and extricated her. "Are you okay?"

"Oh, great . . . just great. What does it look like?" Melanie was so furious she could hardly speak. The fish fertilizer was dripping down her legs after plastering her old denim shirt to her hips.

Deke was staring at her open-mouthed. "You! What in the devil . . ."

"Darling, who is it?" An attractive brunette with a gamine hair style hovered at the top of the steps. She was immaculate in a white sleeveless dress which revealed an expanse of smooth, tanned skin. "What's happening down there?"

"You'd better explain it," Melanie said to Deke. "I can't."

"What makes you think I can?"

As his glance lingered longer than necessary on her bare thighs, she added tartly, "It's a good thing I'm wearing shorts or you'd never have recognized me."

His glance shot up to her face and a grim look creased his features. "You *do* have a penchant for unscheduled appearances in unorthodox outfits, Miss Adams." Then as the brunette came down the stairs over to his side, he said, "Jessica, this is Melanie Adams." He continued with scarcely a break. "Jessica Hendricks . . . who comes up from our headquarters in California every now and then to whip us into shape." As he spoke, he was righting the sprinkler can and turning on the hose. "I'll wash this down if you two will get out of the way. We can have the explanations later. That mixture may be good for marigolds but it doesn't do much for anything else." For the brunette's benefit, he said, "None of it got in the water, Jessica—so you can have your swim on schedule."

Melanie forgot about her dismal appearance as she tried to take the hose from him. "I can do that. After all, it was my fault."

He half-turned in surprise. "I thought you'd want to take a shower."

"Well, of course I do. Just as soon as I've cleaned this up. After all, it *is* my job."

The perplexed expression on his face changed to a sudden frown. "What did you say?"

"I said this was my job." Her hand tugged more insistently. "That water isn't doing the foliage any good. The soil needs it more."

The spray stayed exactly where it was. So did the hose as Deke said grimly to her, "Maybe we'd better have some explanation, after all. Why are you wrestling sprinkling cans here at Tukwila when the last I knew, you were headed toward the beach?"

Melanie wished that she'd managed to change before being forced into giving answers. A quick upward look through her lashes showed that Deke's jaw was set stubbornly. Evidently there was no chance of a reprieve there. She edged into her response gingerly. "Yes . . . well, I changed my mind. Chet . . . the man at Canfield Camp . . ."

"I know who Chet is," he pointed out with un-utterable logic. "Get on with it."

Melanie kept her glance lowered, reluctant to tangle with the suspicious expression on Jessica Hendricks's face. It would have been better, she thought irritably, if she could have explained to Deke in private. "He said that Tukwila Lodge was very nice." She chose her words carefully. "So I came up to look."

"How did you get here?" Deke rapped out impatiently.

"Les brought me . . . Les Roberts."

"I know who Les is, too." Deke kept his voice level but she could hear an undercurrent that boded ill. "Where is he now?"

She waved a vague hand, edging toward the steps. "Upriver. He said he had some work to do. But he'll be back soon. Now that I've stopped dripping, I'll go along. It's time I checked on Obie."

Deke cut in before she could say more. "And I'm acquainted with Obie, so you can skip that one, too. What I don't know is where he's gotten to."

"He's here . . . resting in his bedroom." Melanie swallowed. "You see, he wasn't feeling well. His heart . . . he has these attacks . . ."

"Why in the deuce didn't you say something before this. You don't have to explain to me about Obie's heart attacks. I've known the man for thirty years." Deke shut off the hose with an abrupt gesture and headed for the stairs. "Why isn't somebody with him?"

Melanie was hot on his heels as they turned toward the lodge. "Because he shouldn't be bothered. He's taken his pills and he's resting. It hasn't been a half hour since Les left and I saw Obie just before that when we had coffee."

Deke pulled up outside the heavily carved door and scowled at her. "You've certainly been busy for a casual visitor, Miss Adams. I'm sure that Obie appreciates your help but there's no need to go grubbing in the flowerbeds. Just because the manager is under the weather temporarily doesn't mean this place will fall apart. You'd better get cleaned up," he told her in more kindly fashion as he pushed open the door, "so you'll be ready to go when Les picks you up for his return trip."

"But, Mr. Brandt . . ." Melanie's anguished tone caught him halfway through the big room. "Les isn't going back downriver tonight."

"You mean he brought the cook up this morning? Is Martha here already?"

She shook her head. "I heard him tell Obie that Martha wouldn't be able to come for a few more days."

"A few more days! What in the hell are we supposed to do in the meantime?"

"It's all right. He's hired someone else," Melanie assured him as she backed away. "There won't be any trouble."

"Just a minute." This time, he caught *her* halfway across the breezeway to the guest wing. "Where is the temporary cook? Who's he hired . . ." His voice trailed off even as he uttered the last word and he brought up the heel of his palm to his forehead in a gesture of despair. "Don't tell me ˙. . . let me guess."

"I was trying to explain all along but you didn't give me a chance," her words rushed out in a nervous gulp. "Mr. Roberts hired me—just before he had his heart attack." She surveyed his wrathful face apprehensively. "Now I'll go and get changed, Mr. Brandt."

"You do that, Miss Adams." His snarl pursued her up the staircase and came clearly to her ears even when she was on the second landing. "You can do anything so long as you get out of my sight. It'll be a hell of a lot easier that way!"

Chapter Two

When Melanie emerged from her room a half hour later, her hair was still damp from the recent shower but she smelled wonderfully of white lilac cologne rather than Eau de Fish and her outfit consisted of a well-tailored blue sailcloth skirt and matching tunic top.

As she approached the living room of the lodge, her steps slowed in some trepidation and then she moved ahead with newfound confidence when she heard Les's drawl through the half-open door.

"There was no reason for you to get het up, Deke," he was saying. "Everything'll work out okay until Martha comes. Dad himself told you he's feeling better and there's no high-powered company due for a while."

"That's not the point and you know it." Deke Brandt didn't see Melanie's figure in the doorway. "You knew better than to bring another woman up here and, as for Obie, I can only think he's getting weak in the head. I told him so."

Melanie caught Les's amused glance and realized

44

that she'd better speak up. "I hope you didn't upset Mr. Roberts," she put in quietly.

For an instant, Deke stood as if frozen to the rug and then he turned slowly, letting his eyes roam over her poised figure. "Are you adding eavesdropping to your other talents, Miss Adams?"

"Not at all. I was just taught that it wasn't polite to interrupt anyone in the middle of a sentence." She came farther into the room and stood behind a divan so he wouldn't see how she was trembling. Somehow, she had thought that his anger would have subsided in the interval, but it appeared she was wrong. She directed her attention to Les. "If my presence is so upsetting to Mr. Brandt, maybe you'd better take me back to Canfield Camp. I'll hitch a ride down to the beach tomorrow."

"Oh, no, you don't." Deke Brandt picked up his glass from the bar with a brusque gesture. "You were the one who wanted to work here . . . you're not upsetting Obie further by running out now."

Melanie felt a surge of relief but lowered her eyes so he couldn't see the gleam of triumph. "Whatever you say, Mr. Brandt . . . but you can't have it all ways."

"You'd be surprised." He took a sip of his drink. "I'd suggest that you stop while you're ahead."

Les moved to break the tense silence that followed. "Well, if that's settled, I could do with some food."

Jessica came through the kitchen archway just in time to hear him. "That's my department. I've been looking through the refrigerator—there are plenty of things for sandwiches and the coffee's on . . . it shouldn't be long."

"Thanks for your efforts, Jessica. In the meantime, your drink's ready." Deke held out a glass toward her. His eyes moved mockingly toward Melanie. "Better join us, Miss Adams. Les's already nursing a beer over on the table."

Melanie had an instant to decide that the line between staff and guests at Tukwila was a very fine one before she said, "No, thanks. I'll go and see what I can do in the kitchen."

"That won't be necessary," Jessica put in firmly. "Everything's ready on the counter for sandwiches."

Melanie turned to Les, "What about your father? Shouldn't he have something to eat?"

"S'pose so. At least it wouldn't hurt to ask." He drained his beer and carried the glass with him as he started toward the kitchen. "Come with me, Melanie. He'll be more polite if you're along."

She smiled slightly and followed, murmuring, "Excuse me, please," to the other two who were watching intently.

Obie was resting comfortably on the bed in his room when Les knocked. After a little persuasion he decided that some soup wouldn't go astray. "It'll be a treat to have somebody else carryin' things for a change," he said with candor.

"That makes more sense than anything I've heard around here yet," Melanie told him from his bedroom doorway. "You stay in that prone position and I'll have it here in no time."

When she returned a little later carrying his lunch, she'd added an appetizing dish of fruit to the steaming bowl of soup on the tray.

Obie swung his legs to the floor as she pushed a bedside table alongside him.

"I didn't know whether Les would eat with you," she told him tentatively. "It will be easy to fix another tray."

"No need." The manager's tone had gained in strength. "Les has other things to tend to. Don't spoil him, Melanie. It's time he pulled his weight around here." He picked up a spoon and fixed her with a worried glance. "What about Deke and Miss Hendricks?"

"They seem to be managing without any trouble." Melanie kept her voice light. "I offered to help but Miss Hendricks said she could cope."

"That doesn't surprise me. According to Deke, she's the most efficient secretary in their main office. Practically nothing she can't do . . . and good-lookin', too. Or leastwise she was the last time she came."

"She hasn't changed." Melanie grinned at him ruefully. "With her profile, it wouldn't matter if she had trouble sharpening pencils. I'd better get back to the kitchen—if there's nothing else you need."

"No, I'm fine. Be sure and eat some lunch yourself. Les said you'd been working hard down by the pool."

Melanie shot him an uneasy glance but he was concentrating on spooning up his soup so it was impossible to know whether he'd heard the disastrous consequence of her morning's work. Since he hadn't mentioned it, Les might have decided to save her feelings.

"I was taking care of the planter boxes," she said noncommittally. "Would you like me to prepare Miss Hendricks's room?"

"Everything was ready for her." He put down his spoon with a sigh and leaned back against his pillow. "Think I'll rest a little before tackling any more."

"That's a good idea. I'll leave you alone." . .

His voice caught her halfway to the door. "If you have time, you might throw a little flake food in the aquarium. The cans are right beside the tank."

"Of course. What are you giving them these days for live food?"

"Frozen scallops. There are some in the freezer but they don't need any until tonight. Can you handle it?"

"I think so. My brother had fish tanks all over our house. For a while, we couldn't open the refrigerator without finding tubifex worms and brine shrimp swimming next to the lettuce. Believe me," she smiled at him, "frozen scallops are pure luxury. I'll check in with you later."

When she got back to the kitchen, an untidy clutter on the counter showed that Deke and his brunette had already made their sandwiches and gone on their way. Melanie's cautious glance through the archway confirmed that they were eating out on the deck, sitting side by side on the cement edging.

Melanie had no desire to interrupt that tête-à-tête, so she ate her own sandwich leaning against the sink while she mentally outlined the rest of her afternoon. First, food for the fish tank. Then, she'd make a beeline for the greenhouse and stay out of Deke and Jessica's way. By dinner time, Jessica might need another pair of hands in the kitchen. At least for pantry help, Melanie decided, as she put the meat in the refrigerator and stored the bread neatly back in its labeled box. She had just finished clearing the counter when she heard an impatient scratching nearby. Startled, her head came up to search the empty kitchen. When the sound was repeated some seconds later, she discovered it was coming from the Dutch door leading out to the garden. Nothing was visible through its glass top although that wasn't surprising, she told herself. Not many short people made a practice of scratching at doors and not many animals were tall enough to peer through glass four feet from the ground.

She opened the door and jumped aside to avoid being run down, hastily revising her thinking. The Afghan hound that was loping around the kitchen on a fast and enthusiastic inspection tour looked like a small horse. He gulped down a piece of ham which had fallen to the linoleum and, after that, set out on a second circuit to see if the gods had left behind any more tidbits for his satisfaction. Melanie by then had recovered enough to note his tousled cream-colored coat was grimy and that his paws were covered with mud. After one more lap of the kitchen, the beige linoleum was beginning to look as if the Jolly Green Giant had spent the night there.

"Come here, boy—right now. I mean it." Melanie tried to sound firm as she reached for a cloth to clean either the paws or the floor. Then, as the hound cast a disdainful glance at her, and trotted toward the living room, she added sharply, "You can't go in there . . . come back here, you idiot—you'll ruin the rugs."

The Afghan had a twenty-foot head start and it wasn't hard to follow his progress. There was a circular pattern of tracks in the living room where he detoured by the bar in hopes of further tidbits before Jessica's outraged tones came from the deck.

"Get away from me, you filthy creature. Oh, look what he's done to my dress." The last was a moan of pure misery.

"Alfie! What in the hell are you doing in here?" That was Deke's deep voice.

Melanie, who'd chuckled with unholy glee at Jessica's words, paused prudently in the middle of the living room. It might be better to avoid the field of battle, she decided, and turned back toward the kitchen.

Unfortunately, Deke, with a hand clutching Alfie's dusty neck, hailed her before she reached her destination. "I might have known," he said. "Did you let this clown in?"

"Well, he scratched," she defended herself, "and he didn't wait for an invitation after I opened the door."

"I'm not surprised. He's never had one." Deke had caught up with her by then. "He's not allowed inside like this. Alfie plays in the river on his travels . . . as you've probably noticed." His laconic glance was sweeping the kitchen floor. "This place looks like a herd of hippos played water polo in it."

"What are you going to do with him? Alfie, I mean?"

"What we always do. Shut him in the woodshed and take him back to Canfield tomorrow. If Chet hasn't sent somebody up for him before then." Seeing her puzzled face, he went on to explain grudgingly. "Alfie belongs down at the camp, but he likes it better here. Every time he gets out of his run, he makes a pilgrimage to Tukwila. Sometimes I think it's because he likes to ride back in the truck or downriver on the mail boat. Just like a kid wanting attention."

"But he looks hungry."

"Alfie *always* looks hungry. He's a bottomless pit and the biggest moocher in the county. Don't let him get you dirty," he warned as she came over to stroke the long, quivering nose of the hound.

"This outfit washes," she informed him. "He can't hurt it."

"Oh?" His eyes roamed over her with masculine thoroughness. "I meant to tell you that I noticed an improvement."

"There was only one way to go."

"In that case I can admit that you now smell better, too," he said, matching her grin. "What about your lunch?"

"I'm finished, thanks." She bit her lip thoughtfully before saying, "Getting back to Alfie . . . where's this woodshed you're putting him in?"

"By the garage. You don't have to make it sound as if I'm leading him to Dachau. It's clean and roomy plus having a perfectly good dog bed in the corner. Obie supplied it after Alfie dropped in on us for the twentieth time."

"Well, if Obie doesn't object, I don't see why you should," she pointed out.

He refused to take offense. "Who's objecting? I'm just following the standard operating procedure for Alfie's visits. Naturally he'd prefer a little more leeway but—"

She cut in absently, "Does he run away if you don't keep him in the woodshed?"

"Not that I've ever noticed," Deke said with some amusement. "He's more inclined to curl up on the davenport by the fireplace . . . only I don't encourage him to pursue that hobby, because Obie *does* object. Are you thinking of volunteering your services for another cause?"

"It does seem a shame to shut him up on such a nice day. I could watch him."

"The way Alfie travels, it'd be easier to chaperon a bucket of frogs." At her crestfallen expression, he relented. "Tell you what . . . why don't you take him out for a run a little later. There's a nice flat stretch of riverbank just around the bend. Alfie's partial to it."

Her face brightened. "Fine. I'll make sure to finish everything else first."

"Whoa! Take it easy. If you work at your regular job in this way, it's no wonder you need a vacation."

His hand absently stroked Alfie's nose. "Although why in the deuce you choose to take a working one is more than I know. The hotels down on the beach aren't that expensive and if.you just need to borrow some money to tide you over . . . "

"No, thanks, I'd rather not," she said. "Obie and I have it all arranged." This was no time to volunteer the information that her bank account was healthy enough to cover a month on the beach, if necessary, and she couldn't explain why she wanted to stay at Tukwila. A quick upward glance at his frowning face made her decide that she'd better make an effort. "Les offered to help me . . . " she began.

Deke didn't let her finish. "In that case, I'll stop worrying. He's a good man but don't get carried away by his promises."

"That's what you call being damned with faint praise," said the younger man as he paused in the dining room archway. "I'm not sure I like it." His eyes wandered down to the Afghan, who was now calmly resting his head against Brandt's thigh. "What in the hell's Alfie doing here?"

"You can ask him on the way to the woodshed," Deke announced. "Jessica's waiting to take some dictation, so you can assume custody. Incidentally, she's planning dinner at seven. That'll allow time for a swim and cocktails later on if you two care to join us." He spared a final glance at the dog and then said to Melanie, "Alfie'll be perfectly okay shut up for a while. Probably even welcome a nap after his hike up the trail."

"When does he go back?" Les asked.

Deke shrugged. "Damned if I know. I have to take Jessica back down to town in the truck first thing in the morning. She plans to connect with that noon plane to San Francisco. When are you making the run in the boat?"

"Early, I guess. Why?"

"Then you can take Alfie with you. He likes to ride in the front seat of the truck and Jessica . . . "

"Wouldn't care to have him in her lap. Not with his 'cold, wet nose.' I remember what she said the last time she was here." Les pulled one of Alfie's long ears. "Come on, scourge. It's solitary for you."

Evidently the threat didn't faze the hound because he trotted alongside him as they went out the kitchen door and headed for the outbuildings down by the curving drive.

Deke closed the door and turned to observe Melanie, who was watching to see where Alfie was being taken. He waited until she had moved away from the window and then said, "Les is too hard on Jessica. She just isn't used to big dogs."

He was interrupted by a feminine voice from the front part of the lodge, "Deke! What on earth's taking you so long?"

"I'm coming." He started to say something else but stopped, scowling. To Melanie, he added, "I'll see you later. Let me know if you have problems."

He strode back to the living room. Like a man who had things to do and not all of them pleasant, Melanie decided. She caught her reflection in a

54

mirrored candle sconce and winked solemnly. Things were looking up.

By the time she'd cleaned up Alfie's traces in the kitchen, both the living room and the deck were deserted. She wondered for a moment where everybody had gone and then shrugged. In a spacious retreat like Tukwila a disappearing act wasn't difficult. Deke and Jessica were probably working in a secluded corner and Les would pop up again at will like a genie from a bottle.

She took a few minutes to scatter flake food in the aquarium and afterwards vacuumed the living room carpet. When that was finished, she decided to change into a pair of shorts before releasing their unexpected visitor from the woodshed. A close association with Alfie was hard on a woman's wardrobe.

A little later she knew she'd been wise to change. Alfie took to his new freedom like a "lifer" granted an unexpected parole. Melanie managed to keep a hand on his collar as they went down the steps past the end of the pool and then gave up as they headed down the gentle slope to the river. Alfie bounded off out of sight in the trees before Melanie knew what was happening. For an instant, she thought he had decided to head back to Canfield without waiting for transportation, then he appeared again and shot toward her like a white flash. He slid to a stop, nudged her with that cold, wet nose and was off again, this time in a narrowing circle around her. When they went past the dock where the mail boat was tied, the hound seemed to realize their destination and kept within reach on the rocky path. As the hillside stretched to a broad pebbly bank, Alfie plunged out into the shallow water of the river and came back with a broken tree branch. He dropped it at her feet to start the game.

After that, the stick was retrieved so often that it was worn down to a twig. Finally Melanie said, "No more, Alfie . . . I'm beat. Come on out and dry off. Here's a nice flat rock that's big enough for both of us."

Alfie was reluctant to leave the water but he finally clambered out, bounding over beside her to shake himself thoroughly.

"Thanks, friend. I really needed that." Melanie scratched him under his wet chin as her glance went over his skinny frame. "At least you're cleaner. Did anyone ever tell you that you look like a wet floor mop?"

Alfie nosed her without rancor and then sat down beside her to lick his paw. Melanie brushed some water drops from her blouse and leaned back to face the lowering sun. From the way the breeze had strengthened, the thermometer wouldn't be staying up much longer.

She opened her eyes a little later as Alfie gave a gruff bark and stirred into action.

"Beat it. I just dried off," Les said, shoving the hound away as he came to Melanie's side. "We were expecting you at the pool." He started buttoning a denim shirt over his swim trunks. "If you don't come soon, you'll freeze. Once the wind starts blowing down the canyon, the natives head for a fireplace even at this time of year."

"I'd just noticed." She sat up and rubbed her arms. "It's all right . . . I've been wet enough times already today. But thanks for coming to tell me."

"I'm just a messenger." He grinned affably. "Deke issued the orders. He thought you'd be here when I discovered Alfie had been sprung."

"Mr. Brandt said it was all right."

"Calm down . . . nobody's arguing about that. That's why I brought this along." He held out his other hand with a hairbrush in it. Alfie uttered an explosive woof of delight on viewing it. "He knows what it's for," Les said with a grin. "This is part of the routine, too."

"He certainly needs it." Melanie reached over for the brush and surveyed the panting Afghan. "Where should I start?"

"Either end. Alfie's not particular and he likes the attention, so you can take your time."

"I've never groomed an Afghan before."

"Nothing like practical experience. That's what Dad's always telling me," he reminded her. "Why didn't you come swimming? I've never had a woman prefer a pooch's company to mine before."

"I'm sorry. There was nothing personal." She pulled Alfie over by her side. "I was going to take a walk but the sunshine made me lazy."

"Don't be wandering around this country by yourself. Who knows? You might run into a Sasquatch and then what would you do?" He softened his tone. "Alfie's the only one who manages without a compass around here. The underbrush is high enough to cause trouble, so if you want to explore, get somebody to go with you. I can manage time off or Dad can show you around when he gets over this spell."

"I didn't realize it was such a project." Melanie put a hand on Alfie's neck to steady him as she brushed his luxuriant coat. "Don't worry about it. There are lots of other things to do."

"There sure are. I can recommend the fishing. Right now the steelhead are running. I just happen to be an expert on anything that swims."

She raised her eyebrows. "I'd need one. Other than recognizing a fishing pole and waders—it's Greek to me."

"Lessons cheerfully given—day or night. As a matter of fact, I do even better on . . . "

". . . the night ones. I can believe it," she finished smoothly. "Let's wait and see. I'm supposed to be working here."

"As long as you don't poison his fish tank, Dad won't mind if you take extra time off. And as for Deke . . . "

The hairbrush stopped in mid-air. "What does he have to do with making decisions? He's only a guest, isn't he?"

"Oh . . . sure." Les raked a hand through his thick blond hair. "He's just stayed here for so long that he's used to giving orders. I almost forgot, you're supposed to come back as soon as you're finished. Jessica wants to fix dinner."

"Of course." She started wielding the brush again vigorously, and Alfie wriggled with pleasure. "This shouldn't take long."

Les was staring at the hound. "I'm always surprised at the transformation. One minute he looks like a mess and then the next thing you know, he looks like a buddy of Cleopatra's. It's a good thing he doesn't act like it."

Melanie gave one of the long ears an affectionate pull before she started working on some more tangles. "Seems to me, he behaves more like her court jester."

"Most of the time—although he's moody as the devil if he doesn't get his way. I didn't know a dog could sulk until I met Alfie." Les shook his head. "Speaking of sulking—don't keep Jessica waiting. She can be temperamental, too."

"It doesn't seem to interfere with her efficiency," Melanie said carefully.

"Oh, she's sharp. No doubt about it. And smart enough not to act the career woman when there are more promising things in store."

"What does that mean?"

"Just that she'd be happier managing Deke's career if she had the chance. D'ya notice how fast she volunteered for the 'little woman' role when it came to taking charge?"

"It could be that she likes to cook," Melanie pointed out, trying to be fair.

"I'll wait and see. Of course, with her measurements, a man could overlook some things. Deke could do worse."

"Perhaps you should tell him." Melanie used the brush so vigorously that Alfie turned his long nose to complain. "Sorry, boy," she muttered, annoyed that she reacted so strongly. "You don't have to wait," she advised Les in a matter-of-fact tone. "I'll be along in a few minutes. And you might tell Miss Hendricks that I'll be glad to do the cleaning up since she's taking care of the rest."

"Okay." He brought his attention back but still sounded absentminded as he turned toward the lodge. "Bring the pooch along when you're finished. If he's clean, we let him stay in with people."

Melanie nodded and applied herself to grooming Alfie's feathery tail. When she was finished, she surveyed him with a wry smile. "No doubt about it, sweetie, you must look better than I do. When one man sends messages to you by another and *that* one treats you like a sister—then, Alfie, my friend, it's time a woman makes some changes."

She brushed herself off and started back to the lodge. Alfie, as if aware of his new image, marched sedately beside her, only allowing himself a small lunge toward a butterfly which fluttered within reach. After that brief diversion, he came back to heel and stayed by Melanie's side until they reached the lodge.

The empty swimming pool showed that the party had moved on. Probably even now, Jessica was changing into something glamorous for cocktails. "Nothing like a pinafore apron over slinky evening pajamas for effect, Alfie," Melanie told him. Alfie wagged his tail in response and followed her along the corridor to her room. Once inside, he stalked over to the sliding door by the balcony, waited for her to open it, and then collapsed out on the cedar flooring with a contented sigh. Alfie, despite his pampered features, obviously preferred the outdoor life.

Melanie decided to start looking a little less like an outdoor girl. Not too much, she reminded herself. Already Deke Brandt was suspicious of her presence and any action she took would be carefully observed.

A little later she surveyed her image in the mirror with critical satisfaction. Her coral dress with its stand-up collar and dolman sleeves brought out the golden sheen of her skin and provided a pleasing contrast for her hazel eyes. A matching coral lipstick enhanced the view and, as she poked a strand of hair back in her chignon, she noted that two days in the Rogue sunshine had given her hair some platinum streaks that were undeniably becoming. She debated whether to take a matching shawl and draped it seductively around her shoulders. Then she blushed at such an obvious maneuver and shoved the shawl back in the drawer.

"Come on, Alfie," she said, snapping her fingers at the peacefully sleeping hound, "it's time we made ourselves useful."

Alfie opened his black eyes and raised his head. He yawned and then rose to his feet, clearly reluctant to abandon the balcony.

"Food, Alfie my love," Melanie told him, coming

over to close the balcony door behind him to keep out the cool breezes which were already making a mockery of the setting sun's rays. "Then you can stretch out in front of the fireplace and live up to your image."

Melanie found the rest of the party already congregated in the large lodge living room.

Les looked over his shoulder as he arranged logs in the big native stone fireplace and whistled appreciatively. "Hey . . . I like it. Dad—you should let me recruit new help every time."

Obie smiled at Melanie from where he sat quietly in a corner of a couch. "I think he's right. You're a sight for tired eyes, girl."

"Thanks, Obie . . . but should you be out of bed?" She deliberately kept her eyes averted from the place where Deke's tall figure stood motionless.

"That's what I asked him but I didn't get anywhere," Deke put in.

"You all fuss too much," Obie said defiantly. "I feel fine."

"That may be," the younger man told him, "but you're still heading back to bed as soon as you've eaten."

"That won't be long now." Jessica came to the dining room archway and smiled in at them. She had changed into an ankle-length patchwork skirt which looked bright and cheerful below a long-sleeved cotton blouse. Score one for Miss Hendricks, Melanie decided. Her clothes sense couldn't be faulted. It would be interesting to see if her cooking matched.

"Is there anything I can do to help you?" Melanie asked her.

"I think everything's under control. If you'd like to make yourself useful you could fill the water glasses." Her sweet, patronizing tone showed clearly that the task was about all Melanie could manage.

Alfie started to follow Melanie into the dining room until Deke snapped his fingers and said, "Lie down, Alfie. For once in your life, stay out of the way."

Obie gave him a puzzled look before telling Les, "Go ahead and light that fire, son. It feels chilly in here." Then, casually, "What's eating you, Deke? You look upset about something."

Melanie didn't wait to hear his answer but went on in to the kitchen and set about filling a water pitcher she found in the cupboard.

Jessica moved over to the stove. "As soon as you're finished with that, call the men to dinner, will you. This can't be kept waiting."

"All right." Melanie wondered what exotic dish she was concocting that required such precise timing and, after filling the pitcher, managed to peek over Jessica's shoulder. She was amazed to view a pan of link sausages simmering on one back burner and some overcooked hash browns on the other as Jessica stirred a frying pan of runny-looking scrambled eggs. "Scrambled eggs!" Melanie thought with amazement. And not even appetizing scrambled eggs. From the manner of command, anyone would think Jessica was whipping up a gourmet feast. Melanie kept her expression carefully schooled, however, when she filled the water glasses on the big round table and called the men to dinner a few minutes later.

"Here we are," Jessica said, coming from the kitchen with two plates in her hand. "Melanie, I've put some toast in the oven. Would you watch it while I bring in the rest of the food. The men can start with their juice."

"Of course." Melanie escaped gladly, happy to stay out of the way for a while. Deke, Les, and Obie were trying hard to look enthusiastic about the food being set in front of them but they weren't succeeding very well.

When Melanie came back with a plate of buttered toast and slipped into her chair, only Jessica had made appreciable inroads on the main course. Finally the brunette put down her fork and said accusingly, "Is there something wrong? I thought men enjoyed eggs at any time of day."

"Tastes great," Les mumbled, slathering catsup over them and trying again.

"It's fine, Miss Hendricks," Obie put in. "Those pills of mine take away a body's appetite, that's all."

"I don't know where you get the idea anything's wrong," Deke confirmed, resolutely chewing his charred sausage. "Cranberry juice and plain scrambled eggs are favorites of mine."

"It isn't cranberry juice—I mixed orange and grape juice. And the eggs are special—they have a cup of Parmesan cheese in them. I heard the recipe on the car radio one day when I was driving home from work." Jessica bit her lower lip and then went on.

"Actually I wasn't sure exactly how much cheese to put in. By the time I got home and wrote the recipe down, I'd forgotten what they said."

Melanie took a bite of her eggs and hastily sipped some water. Something had obviously been lost in the translation.

"Well, it was thoughtful of you to help out, Jessica." Deke took a swallow of coffee after manfully cleaning his plate. "We appreciate it."

"I don't know what you'll do tomorrow night." Jessica reached up to push a strand of hair from her cheek. "I really should be back at work or I'd change my plane reservation."

"We'll take potluck," Deke said hastily. "It won't hurt us for one night and Martha will be up day after tomorrow. After that it's smooth sailing."

The Tiffany-shaded fixture on the ceiling cast a shadow over one side of his face. In its reflection, he looked watchful and older than the man Melanie had encountered in Canfield Camp that morning. She waited for him to turn and ask if she'd mind struggling in the kitchen for one day but he kept his glance resolutely on the coffee mug he was holding between his palms.

"I'll be back to normal tomorrow," Obie growled. "All I need's a good night's sleep, before I get back to work."

"You'll do nothing of the sort," Deke replied firmly. "You've been working too hard as it is. By rights, Les should take you down to the beach for a week's rest. Although with all the excitement in town, maybe it's a good thing you're up here."

"What's going on down there?" Jessica wanted to know.

"They're trying to recall the school board for one thing; the citizens are unhappy about a special levy they're trying to pass. Then there's the bank robbery . . . "

"I read a newspaper headline about that while I was waiting for you," Jessica commented, holding out her coffee mug for a refill. "Do they have any lead on the suspects?"

"I didn't pay much attention. I think somebody's in for questioning but the money's still missing."

"It seems strange to read about bank robberies in an area like this."

"They've had plenty of excitement around the Rogue all through its history," Deke said. "The Indian tribe and the settlers later on were pretty tough customers."

"If you don't mind, I'll head back to the bedroom," Obie said, struggling to his feet with an effort. "No, don't get up . . . I can manage fine."

"But dessert . . . " Jessica said, with a frown creasing her lovely brow. "Don't you want dessert? I fixed an instant pudding I found in the cupboard. Frankly I don't like them but I thought you should have something."

"I'll pass this time, thanks. See you in the morning."

As Obie left the room, Deke directed a frowning glance at Les. "Think he needs help?"

"He'd throw me out if I went along now. I'll give him a few minutes." The younger man picked up his plate and Obie's scarcely touched one, as well. "Who's for pudding?"

Melanie thought quickly. There was very little a cook could do to ruin instant pudding and she was hungry. Aloud, she said, "That sounds good. I'll help you clear the table, Les."

"Sit still and eat your dinner," Deke instructed, deigning to look at her for the first time. "We can all carry our plates to the kitchen later on."

"I'll bring in the dessert," Les said, going through the archway.

Melanie took a last swallow, and picked up her plate to put it on the sideboard, hoping no one would notice how little she'd actually eaten. "Oh, I mustn't forget to feed Alfie," she said to cover the silence. "He's been good to wait this long."

Deke got up slowly, deliberately. "Alfie can wait. I told you to sit down and have your dinner." He stood there while she wavered, annoyed that he was singling her out with his orders yet subconsciously grateful for his concern. Les interrupted the charged atmosphere as he came back carrying a tray and three helpings of pudding.

"I took you at your word, Jessica." He deposited the dishes on the polished table with a flourish. "Sure you don't want to change your mind?"

"I'd like to indulge but I don't dare. It costs me two calories just to lick my lips." She shot Melanie a humorous glance as they all sat down again. "I've been dieting for months and I'm just now getting to where I can look at the scale."

Melanie warmed to her. "I never would have known . . . "

Jessica crossed her fingers. "Actually I'm down twenty pounds. When I started out, I took showers in the dark so I wouldn't have to see myself in the bathroom mirror."

"Well, right now you look great," Deke assured her, chuckling. He let his glance move to Melanie. "What do you have on the docket tomorrow?"

"Whatever Obie has in mind. Why? Was there something special you wanted me to do?"

An annoyed expression settled on his face. "No, of course not. I wondered what you planned for your spare time."

She gave a small smile. "I was going to take a walk until Les said that it wasn't safe to wander on my own."

Deke's frown deepened. "It isn't *that* bad." He turned to Les. "All she has to do is stay on the marked trails."

"That's easy!" Melanie leaned forward, her elbows on the table. "Is there anything special to see? On the approved routes, I mean," she added with an apologetic glance at Les.

He shrugged. "Downstream you can hike to Massacre Rock. It's the site of an old Indian battle. Upstream, there's a waterfall that leads into Big Fish Riffle. That's about all!"

"All!" Her eyes shone with pleasure. "It sounds wonderful!"

"There's the old mine shaft," Deke added in a drawl. "Thayer's Mine," he went on in explanation. "An abandoned gold working. It's not far from the trail on the way upstream."

"Do you think that's safe?" Les asked.

"Well . . . " Deke drew the word out, considering. "Maybe not. You'd better wait for company before you go exploring that one," he told Melanie. "There's always danger of a cave-in."

"Get Deke to take you," Jessica said in a new burst of friendliness. "He knows this country like the back of his hand."

Melanie was happy to grasp her olive branch. "Thanks, but I don't want to cause any bother. All I need is for somebody to point me in the right direction. The scenery around here is so gorgeous that most any direction will do."

"Well, we can certainly work something out. There are some other rapids on the river you should see, too," Les said, pushing back his chair. "Want me to feed Alfie?"

"Heavens no, I can do that," Melanie said. She stood up but lingered by the table. "Does he have to go back to the woodshed afterwards?"

"Not so far as I'm concerned." Les looked at Deke. "What do you think? I suppose he could bunk down here this once."

"Might be a good idea. He'd probably bark all

night if we tried to evict him and we don't want Obie disturbed."

Les nodded and shoved his chair neatly in place. "Well, then, that's settled. I'll go along and see if Dad needs anything before he gets to sleep. See you all later."

Jessica rose and started stacking dishes until Melanie reached over to stop her. "No fair. You did all the work before dinner . . . this is my job."

"I'll be glad to help."

"We can both help," Deke said, unfolding his long length.

"No—really," Melanie said firmly. "I won't feel right about staying here unless I do my part. Besides, there are hardly any dishes and feeding Alfie won't take long."

He was eyeing her strangely as if her manner puzzled him. "Okay, if you insist."

"I do. What time do you plan to leave in the morning? I can have breakfast ready . . . " Her words trailed off as he began shaking his head.

"It isn't necessary. We're on our own for breakfast. That's the rule at Tukwila."

"And with my diet—the fewer appetizing smells, the better," Jessica said, smoothing her skirt. "That way it's easier to stick to toast and black coffee." She turned to Deke inquiringly. "Are you going to give me those reports now or in the morning?"

"I'll put them in an envelope so you'll have them."

She nodded. "All right. I might as well go up and pack. Once that's finished, I'll be down again."

"Okay." He half-turned to watch Melanie, who was carrying some dishes toward the kitchen. "Want me to send Alfie along now?"

"Give me a little while to see what's in the refrigerator. I'll whistle for him."

"Just like a Bogart picture." He seemed amused about something but went out of the room without commenting further.

Melanie was thoughtful as she finished clearing the table. Since afternoon, Deke's manner had run the gamut from outright annoyance, to patent disinterest, and on to cool acceptance. Which could be followed by outright dismissal if she went wide of the mark, she told herself. Despite Les's claim that Obie made the decisions, Deke's powerful presence couldn't be ignored.

It didn't take her long to wash the dishes and put the kitchen to rights again. Afterwards she located some dry dog food in the cabinet and had her head in the refrigerator selecting a tasty morsel for Alfie's dessert when Les came purposefully through the door.

"Hi, how are things?" Melanie asked, as she brought out a bowl of leftover beef stew.

"Okay." He looked around and added in a low tone. "To be honest, Dad's starving to death. I was going to sneak him a bologna sandwich or something. He can't stand runny scrambled eggs but he didn't want to hurt Jessica's feelings."

Melanie nodded. "I know." She put the dish of stew on the counter and surveyed it doubtfully. "This has seen better days or I'd reheat it for you."

71

She wiped her hands on a kitchen towel and went back to the refrigerator. Unfortunately, nothing had been added to its contents since her search a minute before. "A bologna sandwich doesn't sound like the answer either. How about something more digestible? Would he eat poached eggs on toast?"

"Would he!" He grinned companionably. "Can we get away with it without making Jessica suspicious?"

"If we hurry. Alfie won't mind waiting a little longer. Here, " she pushed a can of soup toward him, "you heat this bouillon. I'll fix the eggs. They won't take long."

"Thanks, Melanie. I appreciate it. Don't worry, I'll do the dishes this time."

"Don't be silly," she said, pushing up her sleeves before running some water in a frying pan. "This is nothing. I was worried about your father going off without enough to eat."

"Well, this should more than take care of it," Les said a few minutes later as he picked up an attractive tray and started for the door. "I'll do as much for you some time."

"You already have. I'm here, aren't I?" She smiled at him. "Hurry along with that. I don't want those eggs to get cold."

He had no sooner disappeared than Deke came in from the other archway, with Alfie trotting cheerfully at his side. "The pooch was getting restless. I can take care of his dinner . . . I've done it plenty of times before. There's no reason for you to take that on as well."

Melanie realized that he thought she had been spending all her time finishing the dishes. She opened her mouth to tell of Les's mission and then closed it again. Any mention of a tray for Obie would be a sideways snipe at Jessica and there was no need for it. Better to let Deke think that she just moved slowly. She looked up to find his puzzled gaze on the unwashed poached egg pan which had been transferred to the counter.

Deftly she reached over and plunged it into the sink. "I did get Alfie's things out," she said, nodding toward the dry kibbles on the floor. "If you'll assemble his dinner, I'll know how he likes it next time."

Deke's eyes narrowed but he did as she asked. "Once Martha arrives, she'll take over dog dinners. That'll let you out. Or will it? I didn't find out how long you're staying here."

"Obie sort of left it open. As long as he needs me— that sort of arrangement."

He cocked a skeptical eyebrow as he moistened some dog food, pushing Alfie's nose aside firmly when he would have helped. "When we talked at Canfield, you didn't say anything about needing a job. If I remember, you were already one of the world's workers."

"Yes . . . " Melanie tried to find an answer and found an utter blank instead. "Well, things change," she finished weakly.

He put the dog food over in a corner and, as Alfie plunged in, said, "Eat your heart out, chum." Then he moved back to wipe his hands on a paper towel, his attention on Melanie once again. "So you've given up on government surveys."

She smiled. "Not exactly. But this is a lot more fun."

"Grubbing around in a flowerbed and washing dishes? That doesn't sound like a liberated woman."

She put her head to one side and thought about it. "Tukwila has a lot of assets that aren't standard equipment. By rights, I should pay Obie to stay here."

"It's beginning to look as if you'll earn your wages," Deke admitted. "Maybe I was wrong . . . "

She started to smile. "Don't make any rash decisions."

He shoved his hands in his pockets and lounged against the counter. "Oh, I don't intend to. City girls have been here before. They fall in love with the place the first night but by the time the weekend's over, they're down on the dock two hours early waiting for the mail boat."

"Would this isolation suit you the year around?" she inquired innocently.

A surge of red went across his cheekbones. "That's beside the point. We were discussing your part in this."

"You were discussing it. I was just listening." As she saw his lean jaw set stubbornly, she added, "Oh, help! Don't get mad again. If Obie hears us fighting, he'll have a relapse."

"Fair enough." Deke stared at her dispassionately. "Maybe the best way is to keep a safe distance between us."

Melanie was careful not to show the twinge of regret she felt. "Whatever you say." Fortunately, just then, Alfie provided a diversion as he polished off his dinner and raised a dripping chin from his water dish. "Has he had enough to eat, do you think?" Melanie asked as if this were her only concern.

"If he hasn't, he'll be humming around later. Alfie isn't one to suffer in silence."

The Afghan confirmed this by licking his chops complacently as he checked his empty bowl and then trotted back to the living room.

"Apparently he's skipping dessert," Deke said, preparing to follow him. "Anything I can do to help?"

"No, thanks." She wished she dared ask if he meant to offer his assistance from a safe distance.

From the annoyed expression that settled over his face, he must have gotten the drift of her thoughts. "I'll see you at breakfast. Or if you're not up that early—tomorrow night. Obie should feel okay by then." He nodded tersely and left the room.

Melanie dried her hands and took her time about rolling down her sleeves. That way, she wouldn't be apt to meet him again when she cut through the living room on the way to the guest wing. She stared disconsolately out the kitchen window into the darkness beyond. It was a shame that they had to cross verbal swords every time they met. When she heard that Deke was a man of strong convictions, she didn't know that his temper was as short as Alfie's leash.

Or maybe she just plain irritated him. There was a niggling suspicion at the back of her mind that if they'd met for a dinner date at the beach as he suggested, she might have seen an entirely different side of his personality.

When she finally turned off the kitchen light and went through to the living room, she found Alfie as its only occupant. He was snoozing in front of the fire and his head came up reluctantly at her entrance.

"I can see you're thrilled, too," she told him with some asperity. "Ungrateful hound," she added as his chin went determinedly back on the rug. "I'll remember it the next time you want to play in the water." Alfie's tail whacked the rug once to acknowledge her warning and then his eyes closed again.

Melanie detoured by the fish tank, thinking that at least the fish wouldn't argue with the hand that fed them. They might even show their approval. But when the tiny cowfish decided that he preferred a nip of her finger to the squid flakes she was scattering, she decided that it simply wasn't her day.

She went over to select a book from the well-filled shelves on one wall and took it with her to her room. Once there, she changed into a green velour robe and curled up in a chair to read until she was sleepy.

It wasn't until she lowered the book an hour or so later that she became conscious of the silence around her. At Tukwila, like Canfield Camp, the rest of the world seemed light-years away. She stood up then and put her book on the lamp table, deciding that the solitude disturbed her more than usual tonight because she was tired. After all, it had been a long day and an eventful one.

She put on her pajamas and went into the bathroom to brush her teeth. There she discovered that the shorts she'd washed after her mishap by the pool were still as wet as when she'd hung them over the shower railing. The air-conditioning, of course. They never would dry at that rate.

She took them down and went through the bedroom to shove open the balcony door. Outside, they might partially dry in the breeze and the early morning sun should do the rest.

Once the sodden shorts were hung on the balcony rail, she placed her wet canvas shoes alongside. That way she wouldn't stumble over them in the bathroom for the rest of the night.

She stood looking toward the river, which gleamed metallically in the moonlight, and shivered as the breeze molded her pajamas to her body. It might be summer during the day but the nights held the crispness of fall. A jingle from her childhood flashed through her head,

> First it rained, then it blew
> Then it friz and then it snew.

If she stayed around Tukwila long enough, she told herself, going back into the bedroom and closing the balcony door, she might even see that.

Humming contentedly, she walked into the bathroom to complete the toothbrushing routine. She had just finished and was blotting her lips on a towel when a firm knocking sounded on her hall door. She hastily replaced the towel on the rod as the knock was repeated. Any number of things could have happened, she thought, moving quickly to the door. Obie could be worse—or Jessica had changed her mind about wanting someone to prepare breakfast—or Les could have decided against taking Alfie with him. They were all possibilities.

The only person she hadn't considered in the "possibles" was standing in the hallway when she opened the door. Deke Brandt was still fully dressed as she'd seen him last.

"You!" Melanie blinked with surprise. Then her chin came up defiantly as she groped to tighten the belt on her robe. "What are you doing here?"

Her manner brought an unwilling smile to his face. "Well, not what you have in mind, I can assure you. I thought you were the one making the advances." As she continued to stare dazedly at him, he held out the wet shorts and shoes that he was clutching in one hand. "If you were aiming at my head, you scored a direct hit. That wet wash took five years off my life."

"But how did you find it? I put it on the balcony railing to dry."

"Well, next time anchor your laundry with a rock or something. That way it won't go flying off in the breeze." He softened his warning. "Sorry, I didn't mean to get you up. This could have waited until morning but I guess I lost my temper after I got your shoes in my face."

She stared at the soggy bundle he'd dumped in her hands. "I don't blame you . . . I'm terribly sorry it happened. I just can't understand how a breeze could move wet tennis shoes around like that. It wasn't blowing that hard."

"Maybe it kicked up since you were out there." He moved past her calmly to push the balcony door aside. "I don't think you'd better try to leave that stuff out there again tonight. Take it down to the dryer in the . . ." His voice trailed off. "Well, I'll be damned!"

"What's the matter?" Melanie dropped her laundry onto a formica shelf by the door and hurried over to the balcony beside him. "What's happened? Oh, my lord!" She fell silent as she saw the top balcony railing dangling awkwardly out into space, barely connected to the upright post at one end.

Deke, looking suddenly grim, tested the balcony floor with his foot and then moved across it to pull the railing back where it belonged. "I guess I should be thankful that the damned two-by-four didn't come down on me. You didn't notice anything when you draped the clothes over it?"

"No," her voice was without expression and her fingers looked ghost-white in the moonlight as they clutched the sliding door, "but I didn't stay around. The breeze was chilly. Otherwise I probably would have leaned on the railing to admire the view. I did earlier." She didn't protest when he took her elbow firmly and drew her back into the bedroom but she did look up at him with a crooked smile. "In that case, you might have been saddled with more than a piece of lumber."

Deke surveyed the pale face turned up to his and reacted instinctively. His arms pulled her comfortingly against his chest. "It's all right," he said in a tone almost as thick as hers. "There's probably a logical explanation for all this. At least you didn't get hurt."

Melanie raised her head to nod and decided she felt better. She pushed back a little from him and noted that his clasp loosened reluctantly. "You *did* mention that it would be better to keep a safe distance between us," she said, trying for a light touch.

"This comes under the heading of extenuating circumstances," he pointed out, firmly drawing her back once again. "I'm still suffering from shock even if you aren't. Consider it a kind of group therapy."

He felt her slim figure shake with a tiny gust of laughter but she didn't struggle. And when her voice finally came, it was muffled from being lodged comfortably against his shoulder. "I was just thinking—it's a good thing I didn't lean against that railing," she said.

He was aware of a fleeting fragrance of sandalwood as he buried his chin in her soft hair. "Okay, I'll bite. Other than the obvious, Miss Adams, why is it a good thing you didn't lean against that railing?"

There was a soft chuckle and then Melanie looked up to tell him soberly, "The first thing I learned at my mother's knee—was never to throw myself at a man."

Chapter Three

By the next morning, it was difficult for Melanie to associate that interlude with reality. As she pulled back the curtain covering the balcony door, she half expected to look out and see the railing firmly in place. That would relegate all that had happened the night before into the category of horror and fantasy where it belonged.

Unfortunately, the railing was still ajar although wedged into place as Deke had left it. And if the railing weren't a figment of her imagination, then the interlude in Deke Brandt's arms was reality, too.

Not that it could be called a monumental happening. The interlude had been all too brief, she remembered, before Deke had put her from him. Reluctantly? She thought about it and then decided that "reluctantly" was a fair description. Certainly he had sighed quite audibly before pushing her back to arm's length.

"The safe distance?" she had asked.

"The safe distance," he confirmed although there was a gleam in his dark glance that she hadn't noticed before. "Get some sleep. I'll leave word to have that railing fixed first thing tomorrow. In the meantime, don't be tempted to play a Juliet scene."

"I'll restrain myself," she promised. "And Mr. Brandt . . . "

"I think we've known each other long enough to skip the formalities." His tone was calm and gentle as he paused by her door.

"Deke, then. Thank you for . . . everything. It was kind of you." She broke off uncertainly. How did a woman thank a man for putting his arms around her without making it sound like she wanted it to happen again. Which, of course, she did.

If Deke caught the tenor of her thoughts, he was kind enough to ignore them. He nodded in friendly fashion. "My pleasure. Good night, Melanie. See you tomorrow."

The remembrance of that conversation made Melanie look across the bedroom to her alarm clock and draw in her breath with horror. Nine o'clock! And she'd made noises about cooking breakfast! At this rate, she'd be more apt to cook lunch—if she weren't fired in the meantime.

Her shower was brief and she didn't waste time as she slipped into a pair of apricot denims and an oyster-colored shirt. Amenities consisted of running a comb through her hair and a hasty application of lipstick before she was on her way down to the main wing of the lodge.

She wasn't surprised to find the living room deserted except for the fish tank occupants who hovered close to the glass with their own breakfast in mind.

"Later," Melanie assured them and went on to the kitchen. This time she was more successful in finding company.

Obie sat slouched on a stool by the counter contemplating some stacked dishes. He looked up as she paused in the archway.

"If I had a hat, I'd throw it in first," Melanie told him breathlessly. "I'm terribly sorry—I overslept."

He waved a placating hand. "Didn't matter. I've been lazy myself. Otherwise, I'd have done those dishes."

"Don't be silly. That's why you have hired help," she said, moving forward and starting to roll back her cuffs. "I'll take care of them right away."

"Not until you've had some breakfast," Obie instructed her firmly. "We're the only ones around here today so we might as well take it easy. You know," he scraped a thumb along his bristly jaw, "I've had that told to me so often in the last twenty-four hours that I'm beginning to believe it."

"I was going to ask how you felt but you look so much better there's no point in it." Melanie moved over to the stove and tested the side of the coffee pot carefully. "It was nice of you to keep this warm. Will you join me?"

"No, thanks. I've already had my limit." He heaved himself erect. "Deke and Miss Hendricks just left a little while ago so it should still be fresh."

Melanie nodded casually. "He said last night he was taking her to the plane. Does she come up here often?"

"About as often as she can find an excuse." He went over to the sink and rinsed his coffee cup. "She says she likes the place . . . and the people."

It wasn't much of an answer but Melanie was reluctant to question him further. "I see my favorite hound is missing," she went on lightly. "Did he go willingly with Les?"

Obie snorted with laughter. "Alfie's gone back on that boat so often that he gets aboard without even being asked. Les swears he's going to train him to carry the life jackets ashore. Says that he might as well make himself useful since he's getting a free ride."

Melanie smiled over her shoulder as she put a piece of bread in the toaster and rummaged for the butter. "Something tells me that Alfie will be back soon."

"That's a safe bet if I ever heard one. By the way," Obie shot her a puzzled glance, "Deke said that the rail on your balcony gave way."

"That's right."

"Funny thing to happen this time of year." He scratched his jaw again. " 'Course after all the rain we had this spring, the wood could have rotted. I'll go up and take a look at it right away."

"All right. I'm sorry that the bed isn't made. I was so late I didn't want to take any more time. I'll straighten things over there right after breakfast."

"Miss Hendricks's room is the only one you have to bother with. The rest of us take care of our own."

"What about clean linen?"

"Martha can handle that when she gets here."

She gave him a rueful smile. "You're practically

doing me out of a job. There must be something I'm good for except feeding the fish."

"Well, if you could cook dinner tonight, I'd be obliged." The wrinkles on his forehead deepened. "Doesn't have to be anything fancy and there's plenty of stuff in the freezer."

"Fine. I'll get lunch, too. What time would you like it?"

"Whenever it's on the table. A sandwich will be enough." He patted his waistline. "I don't do enough work any more to keep this down."

She nodded. "Then I'll dream up something 'low cal.' "

"Right. I'll go check that railing after I shave. I'm running slow myself this morning."

A little later Melanie heard him hammering outside and she wandered onto the deck to peer curiously up to her bedroom balcony.

Obie noticed her as he bent down to pound another nail. He waved his hammer.

"All fixed?" she called up to him.

"Two more minutes and it will be."

"What happened? Had the wood just rotted away?"

"The nails had pulled out. After this, I'm going to check the rest of the balconies. A body could get hurt bad. Even if you landed in the shrubbery . . . " He jerked a thumb toward the boxwood border ten feet below.

"I know." Melanie's imagination had already explored the damage a fall from that balcony could have caused and it didn't take Obie's warning to bring it to mind again. The specter of that broken railing lurked stubbornly in her memory like a headache which was eased by aspirin but not entirely subdued. "I was lucky not to lean against it. That's what Deke told me last night." Idly she broke off some faded petunia blossoms from the planter box at her side.

In the silence following her remark, she looked up to find Obie motionless, his hammer hanging limp in his fingers.

"Deke was up here last night?" he asked as if he hadn't heard properly.

The sunlight on his face made his features look more weathered than usual. He still wasn't well, Melanie thought worriedly, even as she nodded. "That's right. He noticed something was wrong and came by my room to check." She didn't plan to explain that Deke had been caught in a deluge of laundry. Nor did she intend to mention what happened after that. "I thought he told you," she added.

"He didn't say anything about inspecting it." Obie sounded aggrieved.

"That was my doing. I . . . sort of asked for his advice," Melanie confessed. There was no need to get Deke in trouble when it wasn't his fault. Apparently Obie took his managerial duties seriously.

"Humph." Obie thought that over and then nodded. "Well, it's fixed now. If you have any more trouble, tell me about it. No reason to bother Deke."

"I'll remember." Melanie decided the petunias could manage without any more grooming and slipped back into the lodge. As she fed the fish and attended to the other housekeeping chores, she found herself hoping that Obie would have gotten over his annoyance by lunch time.

As a consequence, she tried to fix an especially appetizing open-face sandwich and salad for his midday meal. The manager beamed with pleasure when he saw it and when he finally finished a dessert of fresh raspberries and cream, he sighed with well-being. "Les made me promise to take a nap about now," he explained.

"A good idea. I'll see that the garden is irrigated," she said, pleased that he seemed to have forgotten about the balcony incident. "Your corn needs hoeing, too. This warm weather is really making it grow."

"Les can do that work later. It's too hot in the middle of the day. Deke would have a fit if he knew you were out in that sun. It must be over ninety on the thermometer."

She smiled with real amusement. "I don't melt and it'll help my suntan. There's no need to mention it to Deke."

"If you want a suntan, go down by the pool." The frown was back on Obie's face. "The garden can wait, I tell you."

Melanie knew better than to argue when he spoke in that tone of voice. "Whatever you say. I'll spend my time whipping up a special dessert for dinner. Is that all right?"

"You bet." He patted her shoulder as he went past her toward his room. "Even Deke would approve of that."

She stared after him and bit her lip thoughtfully. Deke certainly exercised plenty of influence around Tukwila. Probably his mining company paid plenty to make sure that he did.

The afternoon passed in pleasant, almost dreamlike solitude. Toward the end of it, Melanie found time for a quick dip in the pool and then lay on a canvas lounge in the sunshine until her suit dried. The air hung quiet and gentle, unbroken except for the occasional buzz of an insect or the off-key complaint of a bluejay in a nearby tree. The sun beat down with true summer force but it didn't matter when one could see forested mountains on either side with patches of green ground cover to soften the rocky protuberances. Below them, the Rogue meandered lazily around the bend.

What other job could she have found, Melanie thought contentedly, where she was practically ordered to lounge around a swimming pool. No wonder Alfie headed for Tukwila whenever he had a chance! Only an idiot would stay away.

She was in the kitchen later on when Les arrived back from his river trip. "Something smells good," he said from the archway. "No uncooked scrambled eggs tonight?"

"Not unless you really miss them," she replied, smiling over her shoulder. "You look tired."

"It's been a long day." He rubbed his forehead with the back of his hand. "I'll feel better after jumping in the pool. Unless you need some help . . ."

His offer was so weak that he went on to confess, "Dad said to ask."

"You're safe. Everything's under control."

He sniffed the air appreciatively. "I thought it was. When do we eat?"

"It depends on Deke. When does he usually arrive?"

"I thought he'd be here before now—" Les broke off as a car's engine was heard and tires pounded on the gravel by the lodge entrance. "Speak of the devil . . ."

"Well, if you see him first, tell him dinner's in forty-five minutes. I have to put in the scalloped corn."

"Sounds good." He was halfway out the door before he paused to ask, "Why didn't you say you could cook last night?"

"Nobody asked." Her eyes twinkled. "Besides, you don't know if I can."

"I'll argue about that later. Right now, even the thought of food can't compete with a swimming pool. The sun on the river was wicked."

Evidently he detoured on his way to the pool because Deke came to hover in the same doorway a few minutes later.

"Les says dinner's in forty-five minutes. Is that right?"

"Close enough." Melanie's pulse rate which had speeded up at his appearance was still rocketing after his impersonal query. She let her gaze go over him quickly and decided that his weary voice matched the set of his tanned face but even that conclusion wasn't enough to still a twinge of annoyance. From his impassive tone, he could have been addressing a complete stranger. Certainly no one would know that he'd played a compassionate role with her the night before.

Melanie's lips tightened. If he wanted to forget about that brief interlude in her room, she could certainly oblige him! Unfortunately there was no way she could ignore the way her body reacted every time he came within sight. Already her emotions were beginning to feel like a yo-yo.

Deke's voice penetrated her consciousness. "I asked if you'd like a drink before dinner." His weariness had changed to impatience. "What's the matter? Don't you feel well?"

"I feel fine. I was thinking of something else." She straightened her shoulders and looked at her watch. "No, thanks, I don't want anything to drink."

"There's plenty of time . . . "

"That depends on how you prefer your dinner. If you want things to taste right," Melanie made her tone brisk as she moved over to the counter to finish cleaning some celery, "you haven't all that long."

A slow smile wandered over his features. "Underdone or burned to a cinder, eh? Sounds like 'Ask and ye shall receive.' "

"Something like that."

"You must have done a survey on gourmet cookbooks back there in Washington. You don't look like the type to wear an apron." His eyes lingered on her caramel-colored dress with its soft neckline bow. Even

Obie's canvas barbecue apron couldn't hide its sleek, feminine lines.

"If you don't get out of here and stop asking questions, you'll never find out," she informed him in a light, pleasant tone that made it impossible to take offense. "How was it down at the beach today?" she added as an afterthought.

He grinned then. "If I stop to answer, I'll get cinders for dinner and I'm starved."

"Things aren't that critical in the time schedule," she admitted.

"If you say so. Actually the town was in an uproar—that's why I'm late. A man was beaten up out by the airport just before I dropped Jessica off. Between the police cars and the ambulance, traffic was tied up for a good half hour."

"That's terrible."

He nodded. "According to scuttlebutt, the man had just been released from jail. Apparently, the authorities had him in for questioning on that big bank robbery but released him for lack of evidence."

"Was he seriously injured?"

"Not too bad. Nobody's talking about that either." Deke watched as Melanie's hands moved deftly, arranging the salad plates. "Why didn't you say that you could cook?"

She turned to laugh at him over her shoulder. "That's exactly what Les said about five minutes ago. I told him that nobody asked me."

Deke rubbed the side of his nose while he considered that. "Any other hidden talents?" he growled finally.

"Trunks full of them." She rinsed her hands and looked pointedly at the kitchen clock. "Want to hear about them now? I warn you . . ."

"Never mind. I can take a hint. I'll leave you to mind the store. Don't louse up the scalloped corn," he added.

Her eyebrows went up.

"It's a favorite of mine." After that, he went into the living room without a backward glance.

Melanie used all her skill to insure that the dinner she finally put on the table lived up to expectations. A reverent hush fell over the men when they glimpsed her succulent baked salmon flanked on its platter with parsley and wafer-thin slices of lemon. And when she brought in the steaming casserole of scalloped corn, followed by another platter of sliced tomatoes enlivened with dillweed–garnished with sour cream, Obie licked his lips in anticipation. But it took the basket full of corn muffins topped with bits of cheese and chive, to make Deke shake his head admonishingly.

"And you let us suffer through that burnt offering last night! If I wasn't afraid that I'd miss something, I'd take you out and beat you."

A smile flitted across Melanie's face, but she remained discreetly silent as she passed the salad.

"Les, are you sure that Martha's coming tomorrow?" Obie asked hopefully, buttering his muffin. "Maybe she's made other plans."

"No such luck. I saw her today when I was down at

the beach," Les replied. "How about telling her she doesn't have to cook when she's here?"

"Not a chance," his father said. "She'd go after me with a butcher knife. Maybe Melanie could help her out now and then."

"I'd be glad to," she assured him. "Don't eat too many of those muffins—there's angel pie for dessert."

A concerted groan met that announcement but Melanie noticed that, despite her warning, the muffin basket was empty when it finally went back to the kitchen.

After dinner, Deke overruled her protests and helped her with the dishes. "I'm not going to sit around in there by myself," he told her. "Obie decided that Les needed some exercise in the garden after those two helpings of pie. Les wasn't enthusiastic so Obie went along with him as an overseer."

She had to laugh. "That sounds like a good idea."

"Well, at least a practical one." He reached for a dish towel and started drying the silver. "What's on your schedule tomorrow?"

Melanie looked over her shoulder at him in surprise. "I don't know. To be honest, I hadn't gotten that far. I thought Obie would tell me later."

"I meant for your free time," he said impatiently. "You said something about wanting to explore the countryside. I have to check a claim in the morning but I thought you could tag along after lunch."

Melanie wasn't sure she liked his invitation. "Tagging along" sounded more like a handout to a kid sister than anything else. She turned back to the sink and concentrated on scrubbing a casserole. "Thanks, but I'd better skip it. Asking for an afternoon off after two days on the job would put a strain even on Obie's good nature."

"Obie won't mind. You don't have to make polite noises about that."

Melanie's shoulders stiffened. "I mean it. I take this job seriously—even if you don't."

Deke dried the top of a double boiler with a concentration that matched hers. "Just when I think I have you figured out," he drawled, "then you throw me for a loss again. Either you're right out of the Pollyanna books or you're a throwback to Jane Austen. You cook like a dream . . . you potter in the garden . . . and you nurse invalids in your spare time. The only thing you've skipped so far is working on a cross-stitch sampler by the fireplace." He watched a flush spread over her cheeks and added ironically, "So you sew, too. I knew it."

"Seldom in public," she snapped. "Does that make you feel better?"

"Oh, hell, I know I'm being unreasonable." He slammed the double boiler down so hard that it bounced. "But, frankly, Miss Adams, you come on a little thick with such sterling qualities. Obie may be convinced but I'm not."

Melanie was all set to snarl, "I swear, too," when the back door was shoved open and Les stuck his head in. "Dad let me out of sight to sharpen the hoe," he reported gleefully. "I should be finished out there in another twenty minutes or so. What do you say,

Melanie, to a walk along the river? You could use some fresh air after slaving in here."

She smiled back at him, her wounded ego surfacing after Deke's verbal onslaught. "Thanks, Les—that's sweet of you."

". . . but not tonight," Deke finished firmly. "She's already spoken for. Aren't you, my love?" He looped the dish towel casually around her shoulders and pulled her to him. Before she even knew what was happening, he bent to kiss her parted lips.

Behind them came a muffled "Sorry" and the sound of a door closing. After that, half a minute must have passed before Melanie was able to pull herself together. She wrested her lips away from Deke's and shoved back from his clasp with the realization that it was then or never. "What do you think you're doing?" she managed in a breathless tone that didn't sound nearly so outraged as stricken. When he stared down at her without answering, she widened the gap between them by another inch or so. "And what do you mean by telling Les . . . oh, damn! I forgot about Les!" She looked over her shoulder. "Where did he go?"

"I seem to remember a door closing." Deke's voice was whimsical. "It came between the bells ringing and the cannons going off."

"I don't know what you're talking about."

"Liar." He was watching her closely.

"I still want to know why you told him that . . . about being already spoken for. We hadn't . . . "

". . . gotten any further than discussing your

splendid qualities," he interrupted. "I remember. But Les is the impulsive kind around women. It's better to 'begin as you mean to go on.'" His eyes crinkled with amusement. "That's a quote from one of those samplers I was talking about."

"I've heard it before." As the effects of his kiss started to ease off, Melanie's temper frayed. "And I'm perfectly capable of handling my social engagements without any help from you. You're a fine one to talk about Les being impulsive after . . ." she searched for the right words.

" . . . I kissed you?"

"If that's what you want to call it. Premeditated assault would be closer."

He merely snorted. "Don't be ridiculous."

She glared at him. "Well, don't bother waiting around. I'm not going walking on the riverbank with you tonight or any other night."

"Maybe it's just as well about tonight. It's been a long day. I could use some sleep." He yawned hugely and went over to stand in the doorway. "I suppose I should give you credit, though."

"What's that supposed to mean?" she snapped.

"You can chalk up some more brownie points for that image of yours. With a little more training, you'd even be pretty damned good at making love."

Chapter Four

Melanie's sense of duty warred with physical reluctance the next morning when her alarm clock erupted early. Normally, she would have dressed and gone to the kitchen to prepare breakfast for the men but as she lay in bed and thought about Deke's behavior, she decided that he could fix his own breakfast. That way he'd discover that his first analysis of her character was the right one: she was an opportunistic female looking for a free vacation niche.

Once she reached this conclusion, she was annoyed that it didn't contribute to her peace of mind. She eventually was checking the time every ten minutes until finally she got up in desperation. Even a hot shower didn't help and she found herself hurrying into a working outfit of patchwork jeans and a denim shirt.

When she arrived at the kitchen, she heard the Blazer departing from the gravel drive. Les and Obie looked up from their breakfast table in some surprise as she went over to peer out the window.

"If you wanted to talk to Deke, you've just missed him," Les said, "but we've saved you some hot coffee."

"Thanks. I'm sorry to be so late. It must be the fresh air in this part of the country," she said, turning to smile at them. It wouldn't do to let on that she felt disappointed. Especially when missing Deke Brandt was precisely what she'd set out to do a little while earlier.

"No harm done," Obie said, obligingly moving over to make room for her. "Deke's a pretty good breakfast cook. There's oatmeal in that double boiler if you'd like some."

A surge of red washed over her cheekbones as she shook her head, "Just some toast, thanks. I don't care for hot cereal." Especially when she remembered the anger which had prompted her to sling that same double boiler across the kitchen at Deke's departing figure the night before. It was a good thing Obie hadn't been around to see that. "Did Deke take a lunch with him?" she asked.

Obie scratched his jaw. "I'm not sure. Sometimes he doesn't bother. Says it's too much work to bother with one."

Les saw her chagrined expression. "Hey, don't look like that. Nobody expects you to make lunches. Even Martha doesn't bother with them. That reminds me," he glanced at his watch and pushed back his chair, "I'd better be on my way. I promised to pick her up this morning and there'll be the devil to pay if I keep her waiting."

Melanie looked worried. "Is she difficult?"

"Well, she's not as temperamental as Jessica . . . if that's what you mean," Les replied, thinking it over.

"But used to having her way all the same. Like most women," Obie said with a sigh. "Present company excepted, of course."

"I shouldn't admit it—but you're right," Melanie replied. "I'll try not to cross her."

"You two should get along fine," Les said, retrieving his longbilled canvas cap from a chair by the door. "Especially if you show her how to make those muffins we had for dinner last night. You'll have to be careful around Deke though."

Melanie kept her voice noncommittal. "Why is that?"

"Martha might not like having competition—even if she *is* sixty years old. Deke's a favorite of hers. I'd keep quiet about going out with him if you want to stay on her good side." Les was watching her carefully. "I hope I didn't interrupt anything last night."

"Of course not." Melanie could feel Obie's puzzled glance but she kept her eyes averted.

"I guess somebody else had the idea of walking along the river first," Les said, probing.

Obie stood up and cut in decisively. "That's not your business, son. Stop putting words in people's mouths." He added to Melanie, "I'm going to be outside working on the generator. Shout if you need anything. And if you want to leave a couple of sandwiches in the refrigerator, that'll do for lunch. Les probably won't be back from picking up Martha."

"*Now* who's putting words in people's mouths?" Les complained.

Obie paused in the doorway beside him. "One thing," he warned Melanie. "If you go exploring, stick to the path. You can't get hurt that way."

"I'll remember." She smiled gratefully at him. "This is the best paid vacation I've ever had."

Obie made an embarrassed gesture in acknowledgment. Then he turned to Les and said, "C'mon, boy, you can take a look at the generator, too, before you go. I don't like the way it's sounding." The murmur of his voice diminished as they walked toward the outbuilding behind the lodge.

As Melanie buttered her toast, she thought about taking a walk on the track along the river later on. There was no reason she couldn't finish all her work before she left. And if she kept an eye on the time, she could be back to assist Martha with dinner. There were some blueberries in the freezer just begging to be tucked into muffins if the older woman agreed.

The morning passed in pleasant, if uneventful, fashion and she was able to set off by herself in the early afternoon. There was a sandwich stored in the pocket of the jacket she'd tied over her shoulders. If she got thirsty, Obie had assured her the river water was perfectly safe.

It was hot . . . there was no getting around it. The valley of the Rogue was being treated to a blazing summer; the air was filled with sunshine and smelled of baked dirt.

When Melanie found the narrow trail leading through the boulders on the bank of the river beyond the bend, she could even see the dust disturbed by her tread. It rose around her ankles and then settled back again; some spilling onto the lichen clinging to the rocky surfaces and the rest sifting down onto the dried needles and leaves which covered the ground. The breeze that had coursed down the river at early morning had disappeared completely and there was an undisturbed stillness among the towering stands of trees as she continued steadily upstream.

Even the chipmunks and birds must have holed up for a siesta, she decided, and found herself grateful for the company of some bees in the blackberry vines and two white butterflies which fluttered in alarm as she passed. Eventually she found a partially shaded flat rock overlooking a white water riffle and sat down on it to eat her sandwich. Afterwards, she debated making her way down the steep bank for a drink but decided to wait for an easier approach. She tucked the plastic sandwich wrapping in her jeans pocket and started off again.

A little later she noted that the trail was widening as it climbed slightly from the riverbank. Fifty feet beyond, it joined a rough road which consisted simply of a double dirt track going through the trees. Melanie paused there for a minute and looked back down the road toward Tukwila. Evidently this was the route Deke had mentioned leading to the abandoned gold mine.

A surge of excitement swept through her. It would be fun to go inside the shaft to try and find the old vein or even inspect the area the miners had worked.

Then she stopped and shoved her hands in her

pockets. In the first place she didn't have a flashlight and, in the second, she'd been practically ordered not to attempt anything like that on her own. Which took care of the gold mine . . . period.

The sound of a twig breaking made her turn to see if there were a small rodent in the underbrush. Strangely, the leaves of the foliage hung undisturbed and she shook her head slightly in annoyance. The solitude must be affecting her imagination.

A quick glance at her watch confirmed that she should be starting back if she wanted to reach the lodge in time to help Martha with dinner. She remained in the middle of the track for a moment longer. Then, despite the hour, she moved doggedly on up the road. Just five minutes more, she told herself, in hopes that she could catch a glimpse of the mine.

She made better progress on the level surface of the track than on the earlier trail which had wound over the rocks by the river. Even so, she had reached her time limit before she rounded a curve and saw the mine's dark recesses. It tunneled into the base of a rise nearby with weathered timbers shoring the sod behind a makeshift wooden barrier.

Melanie moved on to take a second look at the sagging wood which was used to support the mine entrance. It was understandable that a barrier had been erected to keep curiosity-seekers away; the mine had probably been condemned by safety engineers years ago. It wouldn't hurt, she told herself, to just go over and peek in . . . maybe the ruin wouldn't even warrant a second trip.

She had barely started toward it when she sensed movement close by and looked down to see a five-foot snake slithering toward her over the hard dirt tracks. Instantly she recognized the brown and grayish yellow markings of the diamondback rattler on its body.

Every sentence that she'd read about poisonous snakes immediately flashed in front of her eyes: "Avoid sudden movements—remain perfectly still." "Snakes seldom appear in mid-day heat." "Reptiles won't attack if left undisturbed."

If that last rule were true, she thought frantically, then why was this one coming toward her? Didn't he read the same books?

Slowly and inexorably he closed the gap, his serpent's tongue flicking out warily from that flat head like a direction-finder leading to the kill.

Melanie took one terrified step backward and then another. The snake didn't pause; he stayed straight on course toward her, his long body making a pile of dead leaves crackle as he slithered through them.

At any other time, she would have admired the sinuous grace of his movements, but as it was, the only thing that she felt was pure panic. Knowledge that she could outrun the diamondback or circle around it to escape deserted her completely. She could only stare at those dreaded rattles on its body which sounded the forewarning of doom for its victims. If only she'd worn high boots—if only she'd turned back five minutes before—if—if—if. The frantic thoughts leaped around in her mind like chipmunks in a cage.

All the time she was retreating from the snake, she was dimly aware that she was backing toward the Rogue. But due to the circumstances, she forgot to notice that the bank to the river had become steeper and the grassy spots had given way to a sheer rock outcropping.

The rattler was barely six feet away and closing fast when her shoe hit a slippery edge of granite and she lost her balance. She shrieked with terror as she tried frantically to regain it. An instant later, arms flailing, she plunged over the bank out of sight—toward the relentless currents of the river below.

Then, incredibly, silence settled back on the riverbank as if the brief drama had never happened. The Rogue flowed on, undisturbed.

Chapter Five

Afterwards, Melanie determined that she hadn't lost consciousness for long. When she was able to open her eyes, she found herself wedged into a rocky fissure halfway down the bank. She tried to focus on her wristwatch, but the resultant blur only sent panic through her aching head. Then she calmed down enough to take another look and realized that the watch crystal had shattered in the fall.

She closed her eyes to shut out the sun's glare and tried to think. At that juncture, she remembered the rattler and her eyes flew open again. She pushed up on her knees and looked around frantically but the rocky cleft was blessedly deserted. Beyond, the granite slope was steep and unapproachable. Thank God, she thought, as she turned and shoved back against the wall again.

It soon became evident that the rocky terrain around her narrowed the riverbed, changing the Rogue from a quiet giant to a formidable force in the narrow channel below her perch.

Melanie stared down at the fast-moving current, and the nausea that had accompanied her return to consciousness rose again along with a trembling which wracked her arms and legs. She took a deep breath and started looking around her for the quickest way out. While the fissure was mercifully snake-free, it had little else to commend it. Unfortunately it only took a quick gauge of the steep bank to determine that she couldn't get off her perch without help. There wasn't even a foothold to be found in the fissure, and while the various cracks in the vertical slab might permit an experienced rock climber to scale the eight feet to the top, Melanie might as well have been staring at the summit of Everest. Nor was the route down any more promising; the turbulent white water boiling over submerged rocks at the river's bottom could be suicidal. It suddenly struck her that she'd been in far greater danger on her fall than she ever had been with the damned snake. She shook her head and pressed more tightly against the rock wall at her back, trying to ignore the rapids below. At least, she told herself, she could easily stay in her perch until someone came to look for her. It might be uncomfortable but the sun would keep her warm until evening. By then, Obie surely would have sent out an alert.

He'd scout the trail first, she told herself, peering up toward it. But in the meantime, it wouldn't hurt to yell . . . in case any hikers or rafters were in the neighborhood.

"Is anybody there?" She paused an instant and then called. "Can you hear me?"

The only response was the steady murmur of the

river current below. Melanie waited, not really expecting an answer but nursing an infant hope. When it was clear that no response was forthcoming, she decided to keep calling at intervals; it was the only positive move she could make and would help to pass the time.

A little later, the sun obligingly dodged behind a cloud cover to make her resting place more bearable. Until then, the rays beating down plus the reflected heat from the granite at her back made Melanie feel as if she'd been stranded on a roasting spit. The drop in temperature caused her spirits to soar. When she shouted out the next time, she added a chorus of "She'll be comin' 'round the mountain when she comes" to her repertoire. The acoustics weren't bad and she had just decided to try a second chorus when a cloud of dirt sifted down on her head. Her startled gaze went up to focus on a familiar head. "Alfie!"

The Afghan's dusty but aristocratic nose quivered with excitement as he plunged around on the bank above her, sending a new dirt shower onto her head. Then he let out a whine of frustration when he discovered it would be difficult to extend his greetings in person.

Melanie had no trouble translating his thoughts. "Get back, Alfie! There isn't room for both of us down here." When he cocked his head, she tried, "Stay, Alfie!" in her best drill sergeant's tone.

Alfie looked puzzled for an instant and then collapsed with his front paws and long nose extending over the edge. It wasn't great, he indicated, but he'd go along with the game.

Melanie thought fast, aware that he'd be off and exploring the first time anything interesting stirred. If she could only get him to carry a message to Obie . . .

Her shoulders sank in frustration. Even if she had something to write on, how could she get the note up to the dog.

An impatient "Woof" sounded above. Alfie wasn't accustomed to being ignored.

"I know, boy." She looked up at him speculatively. "Alfie . . . the only thing I have is my belt. If I took it off and fastened it again," she said, suiting her actions to the words as she stripped the stiff leather from her jeans, "I can toss it up to you."

The Afghan was watching her closely now, sensing a possible diversion. "Look, Alfie . . ." Melanie swung the belt by her side to keep his attention. "When I throw it . . . go fetch! Fetch . . . Alfie!" Desperately she heaved the leather circle up over the hound's head.

With a deep-throated bark of joy, Alfie disappeared in pursuit of his new toy. Seconds later, he was back on the edge of the rock, triumphantly carrying the belt in his mouth. He stared down at Melanie, perplexed as to what came next.

"Alfie! Listen to me!" Melanie's voice was strained with tension. "Go home, Alfie! Home, boy!"

The hound paced back and forth, whining in frustration. Then as Melanie made no move to take his new toy, he edged back from sight.

She heard a muffled snuffling from above, and commanded again. "Go home, Alfie! Take it home!"

There was a pause, then a slight sifting of dirt from overhead. After that . . . nothing.

For five minutes, Melanie stood watching to see what the Afghan would do. Until his grimy head had disappeared, she hadn't realized how much she had welcomed his presence. It was a temptation to whistle for him again but she managed to batten down the impulse. With any luck, Alfie might be trotting back toward Tukwila now, bearing his latest trophy.

She tried to remember if she'd ever heard of Afghans acting like retrievers and then shook her head in despair. There probably wasn't a chance of the scheme succeeding—but at least she'd tried. That was all she could do.

For the first time, she felt the breeze which funneled down the Rogue each evening and she bit her lip as it brushed over her shoulders. First heat, then cold. It was beginning to sound like a post office motto. She settled back in the fissure, too despondent to even try calling for help.

She must have dozed lightly because when Deke's call came, it took her some time to realize that it wasn't fantasy. A whistle blast and the words, "For God's sake, Melanie . . . answer me," finally brought her up so fast that she almost smacked her head on the rock behind her.

"Deke! I'm here! Don't go away!"

His answering shout was close. "I'm not going anyplace. Are you all right?"

"Yes . . . yes." She was almost babbling with relief. "I will be as soon as I get out of here. I'm stuck on the bank."

"Keep talking so I can find you." Then, "I told you to stay in the truck."

"Stay in the truck? How can I?"

"I meant that for Alfie." Another shower of dust came sifting over the edge, but this time it was followed by Deke's worried face as he surveyed the rocks below. There was a flash of dirty white alongside and Deke had to move fast to keep the Afghan from forming an advance party. "Damn it all, Alfie! Behave yourself!" His hand caught the dog's collar and yanked him back. Then Deke clearly forgot about him as his glance took in Melanie's tense figure. "Lord, you were lucky!" he breathed finally. "How long have you been down there?"

She indicated her smashed watch with a helpless gesture. "I'm not sure. Too long. I could kiss Alfie," she finished unsteadily.

Deke frowned. "You must be delirious."

"Not really. Maybe I am—I'm so happy to see you that I'd like to kick up my heels or sing the 'Doxology.' Anything!"

"Don't try kicking up your heels. You'd be a mile downstream before I could haul you out of the water." He was surveying the ledge as he spoke. "Can you hang on for a few more minutes? I have some rope in the truck. I'll lock Alfie in." His hand tightened on the excited dog. "Otherwise there'll be one more body to haul out of there."

"Take your time. Now that I know you're here, I can wait forever if I have to."

He grinned. "Settle for five minutes. Don't go away in the meantime."

"If I weren't a lady—" she began.

"But you are," he interrupted smoothly. "That's been the trouble all along. That and your damned efficiency."

"There's another name for my current position."

"Maybe." His expression sobered. "But there's another name for falling off a rock face around here, too . . . we call it dead. Think about it. I'll be back."

It was a subdued woman who scrambled over the edge of the bank a little later. Once Deke had lowered a knotted rope and told her to slip it over her shoulders, it had taken only minutes for her to be hauled up from her perch comparatively unscathed.

"Just some scratches," she reassured him, slipping off the rope and trying not to wince when she felt the scraped skin under it. "I went down feet-first and just had the breath knocked out of me."

"What in the devil sent you over the edge in the first place? These rocks aren't for amateur climbers."

"You don't have to tell me that. I've memorized every crack on the bank and there isn't one that has a toehold for a midget." She was loath to confess the cause of her idiotic behavior but she sneaked a look at the firm line of his jaw and realized there was no escape. "If you must know," she said finally, "I met a rattlesnake on the path—"

Deke cut in tersely. "Did he strike?"

"No . . . nothing like that. I panicked when he came toward me and lost my balance. Afterwards, I must have blacked out, but it couldn't have been long."

"You're not dizzy now? Nausea?"

She shook her head firmly and grimaced with pain as a result.

He reached over to steady her. "Take it easy. I'd better carry you."

"No, please . . . I'm okay. Other than some bruises and a dent to my pride."

"Maybe. We'll see what you feel like after a hot bath and something to eat." He helped her along the road toward his parked truck where Alfie could be seen bouncing excitedly on the front seat.

"And I was going to help Martha this afternoon," Melanie confessed unhappily. "She *did* come, I suppose."

He nodded. "Les picked her up on schedule. Everything was pretty much of an uproar when I got back to the lodge later. Obie had a feeling you were in trouble. Said you should have been back long before." Deke opened the truck door and held Alfie back when he would have plunged out. "I'd better warn you the pooch likes riding in your lap. Shove him off if he's too much of a nuisance."

"No way." She climbed in and smiled as the Afghan washed her ear and shoved his head between them.

"Alfie was my first ray of hope this afternoon. I was beginning to think I'd been thrown away forever."

Deke slid into the driver's seat and slammed his door. "I'm glad he's good for something."

She turned to stare at him. "But I thought Alfie was the reason you found me. Didn't he go back to the lodge with my belt?"

"Sorry to disillusion you." Deke cramped the wheel to miss a fir tree as he reversed on the track. "I found him about one hundred feet down the road from here asleep in the sun. He had your belt though—only now it's chewed in a million pieces."

Melanie buried her nose in the silky ear next to her. "Poor Alfie—well, at least you got things half-right."

Deke spared her a wry glance before accelerating on the track. "I should have remembered that I'm in the dog house instead of Alfie. It's a wonder you didn't decide to walk home."

"Pulling me off that bank atones for your past sins. Besides I haven't the strength to throw anything right now."

"You'll notice that I cleared out the back of the truck before I came after you. I wasn't taking any chances."

"You mean you've had to spend hours looking for me?" She was aghast.

"Naturally. Who else would do the dinner dishes?"

"I feel like such a fool."

"You needn't. We didn't call out the Search and Rescue people. Les went downriver with the boat and I started the other way after we'd arranged to meet back at the lodge a half hour from now. The only casualty was Obie . . . "

Her eyes widened with horror. "Did he have another attack?"

"No, I didn't mean that," he told her quickly. "He was upset but he was sure that you'd stay close to the track. It didn't occur to any of us that you'd have taken a nose dive over the bank. Next time, though, it might be better if you have company on your walks. Either that or I'll have to unearth that long leash we bought for Alfie."

Melanie managed to nod in response, trying not to reveal how weariness had settled over her. Now that the ordeal was past, reaction had set in; every muscle ached and the rope burns under her arms stung when she moved. Even Alfie's leaning against her shoulder made her bite her lips with pain.

Deke must have been more aware of her feelings than she realized because his right hand came off the steering wheel to clamp onto the hound's collar and urge him gently but firmly behind the seat. "Get in the back, boy. If you behave yourself for the rest of the trip, we'll let you skip the woodshed tonight. Even if we have to talk Martha 'round." Melanie's inquisitive expression made him go on to explain. "She thinks dogs belong outside—not leaving footprints on beige rugs."

"You like her, don't you?"

He nodded. "She's a good old soul. Her husband was a crab fisherman who was lost in a storm at sea. Since then, Martha's managed to support herself and she's still as independent as they come." He swerved to miss a series of potholes and accelerated again carefully. "She'll approve of you."

"Is that so strange?"

"Well, she doesn't like most women these days. I wouldn't dwell on your encounter with the rattlesnake, though."

"Don't worry. I'm not exactly proud of it." She sighed and rested her head against the seat. "It seems to me I've been more trouble than I've been worth ever since I got here."

"I might have agreed with you once." There was a pause and then he went on easily. "That was before I tasted those muffins last night. Now close your eyes and relax. It's another twenty minutes or so until the lodge."

Melanie must have dozed off because it seemed just seconds later before her shoulder was being shaken gently. She opened her eyes to find Deke standing by her side with the door of the truck open and Alfie already on the ground, busily sniffing the rock garden in front of the lodge.

"You're a sound sleeper," Deke commented. "I've already been in to alert Obie. He's on his way down to the dock to let Les know. Now, can you manage to walk?" He had his hands at her waist and was helping her out. "I told Martha that I'd get you to your room . . . we'll bring your dinner on a tray."

"That's ridiculous. I'm not an invalid."

He kept a firm grip on her shoulders even as he

agreed. "Of course not. This is just insurance so you'll be up and around tomorrow. Watch those stairs."

Melanie would have protested further if the feel of that hard, masculine body next to hers hadn't been so reassuring. Her knees still had a tendency to tremble and, without Deke's presence, she would never have made it to the corridor.

He pushed open the door to her room and marched her over to the edge of the bed. "Start taking your clothes off. I'll turn on your bath water. After that, it's straight to bed. Can you manage by yourself?"

Melanie's eyes widened at his peremptory manner. "I certainly can. What *is* all this?"

He paused by the bathroom door and a grim expression settled over his features. "I don't plan to make any passes if that's what's bothering you. I should have apologized about last night before this, I suppose. Anyhow, you don't have to worry. From now on, I'll behave like a sedate member of the family."

His deliberate attempt to cheer her fell flat. "I already have one brother," she said. "That's more than enough, thanks."

He opened his mouth to snap back at her before he remembered that he had foresworn such maneuvers and turned on his heel to run her bath water instead. "That shouldn't take long," he said, emerging a minute later. "I turned the faucet on full force—" He broke off to stare at her still figure on the edge of the bed. "Why in the devil aren't you taking off your clothes? If you need help . . . "

"Oh, no you don't." She kept a safe distance between them by scooting to the middle of the bed. "I haven't needed help for that since I was four years old—especially from my family." The last was tacked on maliciously and she had the pleasure of seeing his ears turn red.

"Deliver me from a woman's mind. That's what happens when a man tries to do something out of the kindness of his heart." He yanked the bedroom door open and paused halfway through it to glance back over his shoulder. "Somebody else will bring your dinner up in a half an hour. In the meantime— do me a favor, will you?"

Melanie's heartbeat speeded up. "That depends," she said, trying not to sound breathless. "What did you have in mind?"

"For once, do as you're told. If you're not in that bathtub in five minutes, I'll come back personally and put you in. Either with clothes or without. It doesn't make a damned bit of difference to me."

She scrambled off the bed. "I'm going right now."

"You'd better."

"Any more orders?" she asked sarcastically, loath to give up the fight.

He was starting to close the door behind him but lingered. "Now that you mention it—yes. Try not to drown while you're in there. You've already suffered one shock today and if I had to give you mouth-to-mouth resuscitation, you'd never survive it."

Chapter Six

Melanie was awake the next morning before her alarm went off. She reached over to push in the buzzer and then stretched experimentally. It took only a few movements to discover that she was practically as good as new and she happily pushed out of bed to go over and open the balcony draperies.

A cloud cover still hung over the mountains letting only pale fingers of sunlight through. Leaves of the wild rhododendrons lining the walk down to the Rogue were heavy with dew and the thin trickle of smoke from the lodge furnace was a gray smudge in the early morning haze. Hardly a time to stand around admiring the scenery, Melanie decided. For once, she'd act as an employee should.

Even though she was down in the kitchen fifteen minutes later, she found Martha already in front of the stove busily spooning coffee into the percolator. They'd met officially the night before when the older woman had brought a supper tray to her. Then, she'd simply introduced herself and instructed Melanie to eat every bit of the omelet she'd fixed. The command was issued with a firm maternal air that made Mela-

118

nie nod meekly and apologize again for the trouble she was causing.

Martha didn't waste any time over that. "Sakes alive, girl! You aren't the first body that got lost along this river and I don't suppose you'll be the last." Her intelligent, dark eyes were the outstanding feature in an otherwise pleasant but ordinary face. Gray hair was pulled back in a knot on her neck in the plainest possible style and her cotton housedress was a severe shirtwaist which covered her spare frame but did little to enhance it. Nonetheless the woman radiated such an air of solid common sense that it extended like an aura around her. "Obie should have made sure that you knew where you were going," she continued after putting the tray carefully atop the blanket. "But as long as he didn't, it's a good thing Les and Deke were around. You couldn't have two better bloodhounds. They've spent most of their lives in this country." She stood up and smoothed the belt on her dress. "When you're finished, just put the tray out in the hall. Then you get back to bed."

"You sound like Deke," Melanie said mildly, wondering why he hadn't reported the embarrassing details of her escapade to the older woman.

"We go in harness pretty well most of the time," Martha said with a smile which showed a set of suspiciously even teeth. "He said you'd been doing fine filling in up here. I'm glad Obie finally got some more help," she went on before Melanie could do more than look astonished at the unexpected compliment. "That man! I'm taking him a tray right after this . . .

then tomorrow he's going down to see the doctor. Deke and Les ordered him to do it. He looks worn out." She moved purposefully toward the door. "If you have trouble sleeping, shout out."

Fortunately, sleeping wasn't a problem for Melanie. Her only difficulty was in not dozing off before her polished dinner tray was deposited safely outside.

If Martha was surprised to see her so early the next morning, she didn't let on. "I was afraid the noise of that boat would waken you. Too bad Les can't put a muffler on the thing instead of raising the countryside." She gestured toward the refrigerator. "Help yourself to fruit or juice . . . I'll have some eggs ready in a minute."

"Not unless they're for you," Melanie told her firmly. "I work here, too. It's my turn to wait on you."

"Don't be silly, girl. If somebody fixed breakfast for me, I'd choke on it from sheer shock. If it'll make you feel better, we'll cook our own."

"Whatever you say," Melanie agreed reluctantly, aware that her batting average with the Rogue River set wasn't very high. It didn't take a survey to learn that the natives were a determined group. Or maybe the word was stubborn, she decided with a smile, as Martha proceeded to set two places at the table.

Melanie reached in the refrigerator for the orange juice. "Did Obie and Les eat before they left?"

"Instant coffee was all they'd take. It's no wonder that Obie's heading for the doctor if that's the way he lives."

"Why did they have to go so early?" Melanie took

the juice over to the table and then went back for the butter. "Doctors in my part of the country don't get to the office this early. Or if they do, they don't admit it to their patients."

"They're not so different around here," Martha said in a laconic tone. "Les had to work this morning. He'll drop Obie off at his apartment in town. Les needed the place when he was driving to college every day and since he's landed the part-time mail boat contract, he still stays down at the beach once in a while. Unless there's something better to get his attention up here."

Melanie didn't rise to that. "Actually I haven't seen much of him. I know he's concerned about his father—I hope the doctor can do something."

"The best medicine Obie could have would be for Les to settle down and earn a living." Martha banged a frying pan onto the front burner for emphasis. "That boy's had plenty of time to make up his mind, but I suppose it's not my business. If Obie doesn't complain, then I've no call to. Les is all he lives for." She gave a short laugh and shook her head. "That shows how old I am. It's hard for me to remember that Les is a man now."

"Don't tell me you're raking Les over the coals already," Deke reproved from the kitchen doorway. "How about some breakfast?" he asked, coming into the room and finding a place at the table.

"I can't remember your ever going away hungry," Martha told him with a glimmer of amusement. "You look as if you could use more than food this morning.

What's the matter? Didn't you sleep well or are you ailing?"

He ruefully regarded the older woman. "I can see the third degree isn't just for Les," he pointed out.

"Well, you look like you'd had about two hours sleep. And asking how you are just shows a body's interest. Your manners are off this morning, too. Or don't you say 'Good morning' to people?" She indicated Melanie's silent figure by the sink.

"Good morning, Miss Adams." Deke's tone reeked with exaggerated courtesy. "And how are you feeling today?"

"Just fine, thank you."

Martha cut in, "What in pity sakes is the matter with you, Deke?" she asked, turning to stare at him from the stove. "You must be under the weather. I can't remember your being surly in the morning before. I hope you feel better after some ham and eggs."

He got up to go to the cupboard for a small plastic bottle. "This morning, aspirin might do more."

"Do you have a headache?" Melanie inquired innocently, feeling it was about time she contributed something.

Deke's expression indicated that it was hardly worth the effort. "That's putting it mildly . . . but I'll live." He rubbed his face wearily and swallowed the pills with some orange juice. "How did Obie look this morning?"

"As if he should be taking pills, too." Martha reached over for some diced ham and put it in the frying pan. "At least *he* has an excuse." When she saw Deke wasn't going to explain further, she snapped, "Sit down and put a piece of bread in the toaster. This won't take long."

After breakfast, Deke pushed back his chair and sighed with satisfaction. "Food helped . . . I think I'll make it through the day, after all."

"I could have told you that. Next time, listen to me in the first place." Martha placidly took a sip of coffee. "Are you going to stay around the lodge or shall I fix you a lunch?"

"I'd like to goof off but there's no chance today. There's some acreage I want to sample next to the claim I staked yesterday. It'll fill most of the day."

"Then why don't you take Melanie with you? With Les and Obie gone, there won't be a thing for her to do around here."

"I couldn't think of it," Melanie said quickly, before Deke could answer. "There's plenty to occupy me."

"Like what?" Martha sat back and folded her arms over her thin chest.

"Well . . . there are the breakfast dishes . . . and I have to feed the fish . . . and check the plants in the greenhouse . . . " She bit her lip as she tried to think of something else.

"That takes about half an hour by my reckoning. Deke would wait that long for you."

A smile played around his firm mouth. "Oh, absolutely. I'll even dry the dishes."

"Not in my kitchen, you won't," Martha informed

him austerely. "Last time you broke a platter." Her eyes narrowed. "Of course, it could have been on purpose. Why don't you set the sprinklers outside if you want to be helpful?"

There was no mistaking his reluctant grin. "Whatever you say."

"And Melanie can make the lunch. There's corned beef left from last night."

"Speak no more." Deke shoved back his chair all the way and stood up. "Bring a hat," he told Melanie. "It's going to be hot later on. And wear some walking shoes if you have any. The rocks are tough on shoe leather."

"You didn't even ask if I want to go. Sometimes you give orders like there's no tomorrow."

"Don't argue. If Martha wants us to go—we go." He bent over the older woman and gave her shoulders an affectionate hug. "Isn't that right?"

She wasn't discomfited at all. "Exactly. I'm glad you've the sense not to argue. Poor Melanie hasn't been here long enough." Her look wandered across the table to the younger woman's rebellious figure. "Maybe you should tell her that when Obie's away, I'm the boss."

Deke stroked his chin to hide a grin. "Absolutely right." He moved off toward the living room but he hadn't been gone long when he reappeared. "Alfie's still snoring in there. Better keep him here when we leave, Martha. We'll be going across country and I don't want to have to spend the night looking for a lost dog."

"Alfie'd take a nip out of you if he heard that insult. But don't worry. I'll keep him inside."

It was nearly an hour later before they were ready to leave in the dusty truck. As Deke stored their basket of lunch in the back along with boxes of sample flags, spray paint, and rock hammers, Alfie's howls could be heard coming from behind the closed kitchen door. Martha's smiling face appeared at the window to wave them on.

"She's served as jailer for the hound before," Deke explained, climbing behind the wheel. "Alfie'll feel better when he gets a whiff of that soup bone she's saving in the refrigerator."

Melanie nodded, trying not to be too obvious in her sidelong appraisal of him. Somehow Deke managed to look immaculate even in whipcord slacks and a short-sleeved cotton T-shirt, which revealed an expanse of broad shoulders and strong tanned arms. The thin nylon windbreaker that he'd been wearing when they came out of the lodge had been tossed casually into the back of the truck along with the lunch basket.

"I see you didn't bother with a hat," Melanie pointed out, as she pulled hers off and put it on the seat beside her. "Why am I the chosen one?"

He gave her a negligible glance. "I've had a couple months to pick up a tan. After your exposure on the rocks yesterday, I thought you'd better be extra careful today."

"Does that come under the heading of brotherly suggestion or fatherly command?"

He winced. "From now on, I'm opting out of your family circle. A guy could get killed in the crossfire."

"I'm sorry—it's bad enough that I was foisted on you for the day." Her fingers aimlessly traced the crease on her dark green slacks. "Martha wasn't even diplomatic about it."

"Believe it or not, that was a compliment." As he intercepted her incredulous look, he went on. "I mean it. When Jessica's at the lodge, she's lucky if Martha remembers to call her for dinner."

"Then this morning—" Melanie broke off and started again. "You mean Martha was . . ."

"Playing Cupid in her heavy-handed way. I'm afraid so. But there's no reason for you to be upset."

He really didn't have to emphasize that he wasn't taking Martha's idea seriously, Melanie thought irritably. He'd said the same thing the night before. So decisively that he'd made her feel like an absolute fool. It wasn't necessary to spell it out again!

Determined not to let her irritation show *this* time, Melanie made a production out of peering up at the clear blue sky. "This weather is so gorgeous, I can't believe it. I keep hearing about the rain that you have in this part of the country but I think it's just a rumor to keep visitors away."

"If you were here in the middle of the winter when the Rogue floods you'd believe it. Didn't you see the cement truck overturned in the middle of the river from the last flooding. Somebody stuck a sign on it that says 'We deliver anywhere.'"

She gave a delighted chuckle. "I didn't know."

"It'll probably be there until the next flood." He kept his attention on the narrow track. "Unfortunately, that exhausts the topic of our weather despite all your good intentions. What do we talk about now?"

Her lips curved unwillingly. "Was I so obvious?"

"At least you're better than a bishop I know. Every time he runs out of diplomatic things to say, he comes through with 'Aren't the cloud formations interesting!'"

"I'll make a note to skip cloud formations from now on." She half-turned to face him. "You can't blame me for trying to find a safe topic. We didn't part on very good terms last night . . . if you remember."

"I remember very well."

"I hope that didn't have anything to do with your looking so tired this morning or cause your headache . . ."

"If you keep harping on it," he pointed out grimly, "I'll shop for a cemetery lot the next time I go to town."

"Oh, for heaven's sake, I didn't mean that you were starting to turn green." Melanie refrained from saying that he had a drawn look and there were hollows under his cheekbones that she'd never noticed before. Perhaps most obvious of all was his air of honed tenseness, despite his obvious attempt to cover it. She wondered if Obie's deteriorating health was the reason for it.

It finally penetrated her thoughts that he'd said something and was waiting for an acknowledgment. "I beg your pardon?" she said hurriedly.

"I just asked if we could go back to discussing the

weather. That was before you launched into meditation."

A gurgle of laughter escaped her. "Sorry, I'll try to do better."

"If you don't, I'll drop you off and make you walk back."

"You can't—I'm lost already. We've turned off the main track, haven't we?"

"This is an old logging trail that goes to the top of the ridge. I'll do the rest on foot—it shouldn't take me long to check the claim I staked yesterday. You can wait in the truck for that part and come along after lunch. There's some rock sampling to be done that's closer to the road."

Her expression was eager as she turned to face him. "Just so I don't miss everything. And you'll have to explain it because it's all new to me. I gather we're not about to stumble over anything like the Alaskan gold rush?"

"You're so right." He grinned. "In the first place, we're looking for copper. If you're interested in gold, you'll have to visit that abandoned shaft down by the river. You were practically on top of it yesterday."

"I know," she acknowledged ruefully. "I'd just sighted it when the rattlesnake came along. Otherwise, I probably would have gone and peeked in."

"Just as well you waited. The timbers in the shaft are rotting in places. You'd better have company when you go inside."

"So two of us could be buried under the rocks . . ."

"Something like that."

"Then I'll ask Alfie to keep me company. At least he could dig for help."

Deke gave her a speaking glance. "I hope you don't attempt anything so damned foolish. Survival is a business in these wilderness areas. The trouble with you is that you don't take things seriously enough." As she stared pointedly at the cloud formations which were assembling over the mountain chain to their right, he broke off in mid-sentence and started to laugh. "Sorry, I walked right into that one."

"I'm glad to know I'm not the only imbecile around," she told him frankly. "After my fiasco yesterday, I'm a reformed woman."

"Don't change too drastically . . . there were some advantages to the old model."

His tone didn't give anything away but Melanie suddenly felt a flutter in her breast and she took a deep breath to subdue it. With a man as wary as Deke Brandt, a woman didn't look for hidden meanings. Probably he simply was being polite. So when she said, "Seriously, what does a field geologist do?" there was only a courteous interest in her tone. "I gather that it's scarcely a white collar job."

"Most of the time, there's no collar at all. It's only because you're along that I bothered with a shirt today. Although we'll need long sleeves or a windbreaker if we get into the underbrush. It's so thick and high in this part of the country that you have to be sure your compass is working properly." He didn't miss the sudden look of concern that went over her features.

"Don't worry, it is. Besides, you won't be going far afield."

"What happens when you do?"

"Nothing very exciting. At this point, a geologist is looking for a promising rock area. When he finds it, he picks a sample and breaks it with a rock hammer ... like one of those in the back," he said, jerking his head toward the pile of equipment behind them.

"There must be a reason for that."

"There is," he continued amiably. "The object is to get a fresh surface on the rock so it can be examined with a hand lens. If it has possibilities, then the assorted characteristics of the piece are noted on a ledger sheet, and the location is plotted on a map."

"That sounds like a lot of work."

"It's just begun," he informed her. "After that, the sample is put in a cloth bag and the label is marked with the number and type of the sample, plus lab instructions for analyzing. Then we mark the area with a piece of pink flagging tape tied to the branch of a nearby tree. Underground, it's roughly the same procedure except that the geologist leaves a metal tag exactly where the sample is found—otherwise there can be problems later on." He changed gears as the trail started to climb through a thickly forested hillside.

"All that for one rock sample," she mused. "I didn't realize . . ."

"When we find something interesting—it's worth the trouble."

"I can imagine." She watched his profile. "Have you always worked in this area?"

Deke shook his head. "A field geologist is worse than a traveling salesman. When I first started with the company, they had a nickel laterite project farther east. After that, I worked in Canada and South America . . . but this is home base." As he eased the truck around a sharp switchback on the dirt trail, it was plain to see that he was as expert in the mountains as Les was with his jet boat on the river.

She stared thoughtfully out at the quiet forest beside them.

Deke let the silence go unchallenged for a while. Then he asked, "What's the matter? Did I put you to sleep?"

"Of course not. I was just thinking . . ." Her voice trailed off.

"Go right ahead but in the meantime—how about breaking out that thermos. I could use some coffee."

"All right." Melanie rummaged behind the seat and found the coffee while he pulled up on the track where it was wide enough for reversing.

He accepted a steaming cup after he'd turned off the ignition. "It shouldn't take me long to check the claim post. We can move back closer to the river when we have our lunch."

"That sounds good." She was regarding him thoughtfully. "I didn't realize you were a man of so many parts."

The thought seemed to amuse him. "No more than anyone. I could say the same thing about you. I wondered this morning whether you were going to be the gourmet cook from Tukwila or the woman who pulled shower fittings apart with her bare hands at Canfield. I must admit that when you were running around the camp in a bath towel, I didn't realize you were such a paragon."

"It wasn't a bath towel . . ."

"Don't quibble. You know what I mean." He reached over to capture her chin in his fingers as he stared quizzically at her. "It's a wonder that your boss back in the Pentagon or wherever didn't put a tattoo on you before you headed west."

Melanie scarcely breathed in his grasp, feeling like the mongoose who discovered his next-door neighbor was a cobra. "I . . . I don't know what you mean," she got out finally.

"That's how the Rogue Indians used to mark their squaws around here at the time of the Gold Rush. Three vertical lines on the chin were supposed to make the women less attractive to the miners and more interested in the braves around the campfire."

"Nowadays," she said with some acidity, "women prefer a reverse procedure. Men should try filing a claim before staking it."

He looked amused. "So, you'd have a man observe all the formalities? Maybe even haul out a book of sonnets so he could properly describe those eyes of yours . . ." His lean fingers tilted up her chin even farther as he let his glance linger. "How they sparkle like polished cairngorms most of the time. Then he could go on to mention how your hair gleams like pale morning sunlight on the river. Is that what you had in mind? Or would you rather he described that figure of yours? All soft curves and such silken skin that it's hard for a man to keep his hands where they belong." He felt her stiffen and seemed amused when she didn't answer. Then his hand dropped back to his side as he sat upright again and said gruffly, "Now what's the matter? You weren't taking that nonsense seriously, were you?"

"Heavens no!" She managed a creditable laugh although her heart was still pounding so hard that it was a wonder he couldn't hear it. "There isn't a man I know who could say such things with a straight face these days. And if *you* tried it, I'd suspect you'd been out in the sun too long."

"Thanks a lot."

She was unaccountably pleased at his reaction. "Besides, I've had enough surprises on this trip without poetry at a picnic. Imagine finding a gorgeous place like Tukwila in the middle of the wilderness! And I'll never forget my first glimpse of Alfie—sighting him out here was like discovering the Queen of Sheba in a kayak on the river."

Deke chuckled. "Alfie is a law unto himself. He's homesteaded the lodge for so long that I think we'll have to adopt him."

"Lucky Alfie. I'd like to be in his shoes."

"That's what you think now." Deke was staring into his coffee cup. "Wait until it rains—you'll be hitching a ride back to town on the first log floating downstream."

Melanie could have cried at his impersonal tone but

she was determined not to show it. "I'm aware of the differences. This is all completely foreign to me." She waved toward the idyllic scene around them. Her gesture took in the towering trees with green banks of salal cloaking their roots; even the perky ground squirrel who was poised on a moss-covered rock nearby. He surveyed them nonchalantly before he disappeared with an abrupt flick of his bushy gray tail. Melanie watched him go and then turned back to Deke. "This country is like a page from the Lewis and Clark journals . . . one hundred years and six thousand miles away from everything I know. Have known all my life."

"Why worry about it?" His voice was flintlike. "You're just here on a vacation. When you go home, you can start taking surveys with both hands."

"That isn't funny."

"No, it isn't. Forget that I said it." He suddenly sounded tired of the whole thing and swallowed the rest of his coffee, obviously anxious to be on his way. "There's some reading material in the glove compartment," he said, as he handed his cup to her and opened the truck door beside him. "Stuff from the historical society in Gold Beach."

"You don't have to furnish pamphlets on how to get along with the natives just to make your point."

"That wasn't my intention," he said stiffly. "I thought they might help pass the time while you're alone here." It was obvious that he didn't appreciate her attempt at humor but he was too well-bred to say so. He contented himself with "Don't wander around," before disappearing among the trees.

Melanie sipped her coffee thoughtfully after he'd left. As always, the minute that he disappeared she felt a familiar sense of loss coupled with the knowledge that her nerve ends would start fraying the instant he reappeared. Which didn't make sense, she told herself, and pulled out a book from the glove compartment so that she wouldn't be tempted to analyze her behavior further.

By the time Deke returned forty-five minutes later, she had resolved to keep the conversation on a pleasant, noncombative bent for the rest of the day. Deke's casual and pleasant manner showed that he had made the same resolution while he was checking his claim stakes and tramping the hillside.

After a picnic that was painfully polite, things gradually relaxed and became more normal. Melanie was given a lesson in field geology as she trailed at Deke's side, asking questions or just enjoying the unspoiled scenery in silence while he scouted for rock samples. The last part of the afternoon he put her to work as his assistant, keeping records and writing out the required label data while he flagged the closest tree branch with a pink marker.

"Where do I go to apply for a permanent job?" she teased when he complimented her on her neat handwriting and numbers. "It's obvious I have a talent for this type of thing."

"More fun than surveys, eh?"

"No comparison. And if you let me tag the branches, too, you could go on ahead and get more done."

He bestowed a sidelong glance. "That remark had bureaucratic overtones."

"So it did," she said, smiling. "You just want me to admit that I'd like to play with the pretty pink ribbons. I promise to be very careful."

"Okay, I know when I'm beaten." He handed her the roll of flagging tape. "Don't forget to fasten it securely."

It was Melanie's determination to follow his orders to the letter that caused trouble a few minutes later. She had clambered onto a rock to flag a sturdy Douglas fir branch and was intent on jumping off when her boot slipped and lodged in a crack just above the ground. Fortunately, she was able to keep her balance but when she tried to move, she discovered her foot was wedged between the rock surfaces.

Deke looked over his shoulder and saw her struggling. "What happened?" he asked, starting back.

"Not much. My boot's caught." Her words were punctuated by her efforts to extricate herself. "I can't get enough leverage on it and there won't be any skin on my knuckles if I try to loosen the laces."

He sized up the situation quickly. "Looks like you'll have to go out the way you went in. I'll get above you and hoist you up."

They were both so intent that neither of them paid any attention to the rough snag angling out from the tree trunk above them. At least, not until Deke put his hands under Melanie's arms and pulled upward. At the exact moment her boot emerged like a cork from a wine bottle, she heard an exclamation of pain and Deke's grasp loosened momentarily. She was able to scramble down unaided, with Deke slithering beside her an instant later.

When she saw the set expression on his face as he clutched the top of his shoulder, she grabbed his free arm. "What's the matter? Are you all right? Tell me what happened."

"How can I if you won't let me get a word in?" He was trying to move his shoulder as he spoke. "It was a damn fool thing for me to do. I should have been paying attention." As she still stared anxiously at him, he added in disgust, "I collided with a snag, that's all. Probably my shirt got the worst of it."

"Let me see." Worry made her voice as curt as his. "Can you sit on that log?"

"Certainly I can." Reluctantly, he let himself be led. "The damage is at the other end," he told her, sitting down. "You weren't listening to me."

She ignored his complaint, intent on gently pulling apart his torn T-shirt. "It looks as if you'd lost a round in a lion's cage, but I think it's mainly surface damage. The scratches are bleeding, though. You'd better take off this shirt or it'll be a complete mess."

He did as she suggested, wincing as he raised his arms. "It's a write-off anyhow," he said, surveying it disgustedly.

"Is there a first-aid kit in the truck?"

"Yes, but you don't have to bother with anything. I can take care of it back at the lodge." He gathered his equipment and motioned her ahead of him toward the road.

"Don't be absurd. At least, let me get the pieces of dirt and bark out of it. Where's that kit?"

"By the spare tire." He was shoving his hammer behind the seat and putting their bagged rock samples carefully in a corrugated box. "What did you do with the tape?"

She handed it to him and her clip board of records before leaning in the back of the truck to pull out a metal first aid box. "I think you'd better get in on the passenger side. I can't do much with the steering wheel in the way. And don't lean against anything . . . you don't want to get any more dirt in those scratches."

He moved slowly but complied, turning to present a broad, tanned back to her as she climbed in the driver's side, clutching the first aid box.

There was silence for several moments as she unwrapped sterile gauze and tried to clean the grazes before applying antiseptic.

Deke winced involuntarily as the cool liquid hit his back.

"Sorry—I should have warned you." Melanie was glad that he couldn't see the way her hand trembled as she daubed at the ugly scratches on his skin. The movement of his shoulder muscle under her fingers made her jerk. "I'm trying to be gentle," she explained tremulously.

"You're not hurting me," Deke's voice was unexpectedly deep. "How much longer is this going to take?" he growled a moment later.

"I'm almost finished."

"I hope so." He moved restlessly on the seat until she made a noise of protest. "I should have known that you had a Red Cross first-aid course tucked away in your background," he added irritably. "You do, don't you?" he persisted when she didn't answer.

She sighed and closed the metal box. "You make it sound like a crime. I also took a course in Shiatsu Massage . . . in case your shoulder muscles start bothering you later on." Then, when he would have gotten out of the truck, she added hastily, "You'd better let me drive. Otherwise you'll start that bleeding again."

"Can't you stick something on it? There are some Band-Aids in that box."

"You'd look a little silly with two dozen of them decorating your back." Her own temper was slipping. "For heaven's sake, Deke, close the door. I'm a perfectly capable driver. I have a certificate for that, too—from the Red Cross Motor Corps."

Deke's only response was to slam his door with considerably more force than necessary.

After that, they didn't bother with any more conversation for the rest of the trip to the lodge. For the first twenty minutes, Melanie was glad of it. During the next fifteen, however, her conscience began to bother her. Granted, Deke was being unreasonable in his attitude, but at least he had an excuse for his bad temper. His back must be feeling as if it were on fire by now, she decided, sneaking a look at his set profile.

Small wonder that he was in the mood for taking verbal swipes at her.

When the chimney of the lodge came into view, Melanie tried to soften his anger. "Thank you for taking me along today," she ventured carefully. "I really enjoyed it. If you need any help copying those records—"

Deke cut in with a resigned tone. "I know . . . you type, too."

Diplomacy went out the window and Melanie's eyes started to blaze. She decided if he said one more word, she'd personally add to his injury list.

He followed her line of thought without trouble. "I wouldn't try it," he advised coolly. "You're still ahead but I play dirty. Just park there by the lodge . . . I'll put the truck away later. And if you're as smart as you appear to be, you'll forget all this." He waved a hand toward the surrounding country. "This is a great place to visit—but you'd hate like hell to live here." He started to open his door. "That's as close as you'll get to any apology from me today."

She stared at him, the effects of his brusque dismissal showing in her pale face. "I didn't expect an apology," she said quietly as he lingered by the side of the truck. "Most of it was my fault . . ."

He made a rude noise and started to say, "You're right about that," when he was interrupted by a familiar voice from the lodge doorway.

"Deke! You're late . . . I thought you were going to be here to meet me," Jessica said, hurrying down the steps toward him. She was cool and trim in an ivory shantung dress which contrasted marvelously with her skin and dark hair.

His face lit up for the first time in an hour. "Jessica —you're just the tonic that I needed. Have you been here long?"

"Long enough. I brought those Arizona reports that you wanted." She moved closer to the truck. "Why, Melanie . . . you're so quiet I hardly noticed you. Martha said that Deke would probably run your legs off if he had the chance. Is that what happened?"

"Nothing so drastic." Melanie managed to smile. "Did you have a good flight?"

"The usual."

"Doesn't anybody care about me?" Les asked, strolling through the lodge door. Then he got a view at Deke's back and whistled, "For pete's sake, what happened to you?"

"Nothing very vital." Deke grimaced as Jessica made a sound of distress as well. "It certainly won't keep me from having a drink and something to eat," he went on. "How long until dinner?"

"It's up to you," Les said. "Martha's in the kitchen feeding the hound now. Claims he gets under her feet otherwise when she's cooking. She wants to know what time you want dinner on the table."

"I can be ready in about an hour. That'll give me time to clean up and—" he broke off with a frown. "Where's your dad? Isn't he here?"

The other shook his head. "I left him at the beach. The doc had some tests he wanted to finish. It's all right, though. So far, they haven't turned up anything new."

"I guess that's something." Deke bundled his T-shirt in one hand and reached for his jacket on the seat of the truck. His glance raked over Melanie's still quiet figure behind the wheel. "If dinner's in an hour, you'd better lie down and get some rest first. You could probably use it." Then, without waiting, he turned and took Jessica's elbow. "Come on, honey. You can make me a drink while I clean up. Something strong, tall, and full of ice."

Her protest floated back. "But, Deke . . . those scratches! They need to be bandaged or something."

"I can slap some adhesive on them," Les said, following them up the lodge steps after a puzzled look toward the truck. "I'll get the first-aid box and bring it up to your room after I tell Martha about dinner."

"Thank heavens you're here," Jessica said to him. "I'm a total loss when it comes to blood and gore."

Deke reassured her, "That's all right. You have a lot of talents that I like better."

Her voice rose with pleasure. "That's the nicest thing I've heard all day. Tell me more."

"I will—just give me time." He paused in the doorway and looked over his shoulder to make sure that Melanie had heard. He stared at her and then, as if satisfied, turned and followed Jessica into the lodge.

Chapter Seven

Considering the events of that afternoon, Melanie certainly didn't expect to find herself housed in a leading Gold Beach hotel twenty-four hours later with Deke and Jessica occupying the rooms on either side of her.

Their general exodus from Tukwila had come about because Deke found it necessary to make a series of long distance calls to his home office after conferring with Jessica the night before. Transportation downriver was no problem either because Les had planned to take his boat back to the beach the next morning and see if Obie could come home.

Melanie found herself included in the group after Martha thrust a shopping list at her, saying that neither Les nor his father ever seemed to buy what a woman needed in the kitchen. When Melanie pointed out that Jessica would be at the beach, Deke had cut in coldly to say that Jessica had other things to do. Melanie would have protested further but she'd taken a look at the determined set of his chin and subsided. When she asked Martha meekly if there were anything

143

she needed besides groceries, the glint in Deke's eyes showed that he wasn't unaware of his victory.

Melanie had packed a long skirt in her overnight bag after Jessica stopped by her room to report that there would be dinner dancing at the ocean-front hotel. "Deke doesn't know it yet," she announced, "but there's no reason why we can't have some social life. Les agrees with me. And with a foursome, it'll work out perfectly."

"Deke may not feel like dancing," Melanie had responded. "His back must still be painful."

"Well, we'll find out." Jessica lowered her voice. "Les is arranging for a doctor to look at those scratches when Deke goes to visit Obie at the clinic. But that's under wraps, too." She shrugged lightly. "It's the easiest way. Otherwise Deke would flatly refuse to see a doctor and we'd be back to round one."

"Whatever that mining company pays you—it's not enough," Melanie told her admiringly.

Jessica laughed. "Don't worry. My salary's another thing I don't let them forget. Hurry up with your packing. The men want to leave in fifteen minutes and it's safer not to cross Deke this morning. I haven't seen him so irritable since the time he flew to Rio for a meeting and his luggage arrived four days later. Usually he's as even-tempered as they come." She paused before closing the door behind her. "What happened between you two yesterday afternoon?"

"Not much. Deke was rescuing me when he hurt his back." Melanie didn't want to go into greater detail but she could see the secretary wasn't convinced by her bare-bones explanation.

"Deke's not the type to be annoyed by something like that," Jessica said finally, confirming Melanie's suspicions. "There must have been more to it."

"Nothing important." Melanie put a small zipper bag with her toilet articles into her suitcase. "I'm like the man who came to dinner . . . Deke would like to send me on my way but he's too polite to do it." She glanced at the other woman. "You're more his type. It was obvious last night."

"That little demonstration on the steps?" Jessica shook her head. "Don't be silly. After I fixed him a drink, he read the reports I brought and then dictated letters for two hours after dinner."

Melanie stared at her uncomprehendingly. "Nothing more?"

"Nothing—but there's hope yet. I'll see what happens at the beach. If I don't get any response with the red lace dress I'm taking along, I'll tell Les to take Deke to a psychiatrist at the clinic." She poked her head around the edge of the door. "On the other hand, maybe I'll need a psychiatrist more than he will."

They had set off for the jet boat ride down the river shortly afterwards with Martha waving at them from the terrace while Alfie cavorted happily through a bed of marigolds at her feet. It was just as well Obie wasn't along, Melanie thought. Seeing all those flowers bite the dust would have sent him into shock once more.

The ride down the Rogue was almost as exhilarating as her first trip in the fast boat. This time, Les invited her to sit beside him at the stern while Jessica and Deke occupied places in the bow. Once they arrived at Gold Beach, the three of them took a cab downtown after Les promised to meet Deke at Obie's clinic that afternoon.

Registering at the hotel was a brief formality. Since it was mid-week, they were able to have rooms with a gorgeous view of the breakers and driftwood-strewn beach. Deke disappeared into his room without comment and shortly afterward the sound of a typewriter could be heard coming through Jessica's door. Melanie combed her hair and then since no orders were forthcoming, she set out to take care of Martha's shopping list.

Lunch consisted of a bowl of clam chowder which she consumed by herself at a tiny seafood restaurant. If she'd gone back to the hotel, probably Deke would have felt responsible for seeing that she didn't starve to death. Defiantly, she ordered a piece of lemon meringue pie so she could truthfully report that there was no chance of malnutrition setting in.

When she'd finished her errands and window-shopped the entire length of the main street, she went back to the hotel. She used a side entrance rather than going through the lobby and quietly slipped into her room to change her clothes.

There were advantages to being *persona non grata*, she told herself with a rueful smile as she put on her jeans. One of them was having the rest of the afternoon to beachcomb through the driftwood and walk barefooted in the sand. There wasn't even enough time to be lonely or reflect on that other invitation to the beach that Deke had issued at Canfield Camp. Although she knew if she'd accepted that one, she wouldn't now be staring in her mirror at a wan creature who looked more like the guest of honor at an Irish wake than a woman on a holiday at the beach.

Her long, leisurely walk along the shore with a brisk wind in her face eventually brought color to her cheeks but evidently not enough.

When she got back to the hotel, Deke's door was open and he appeared in the hallway by the time she had the key in her lock.

"I wondered where you'd gone," he announced, pulling off a pair of reading glasses as he spoke. "Most people leave word with somebody if they're going to disappear for the day—as a common courtesy. I suppose you had your reasons, though."

"I'm sorry—I didn't mean to inconvenience anyone. It didn't occur to me that you'd be interested. I just picked up the things on Martha's list and went for a walk on the beach." She kept her voice low and her gaze on the glasses swinging idly from his hand.

How little she knew about him, she thought, not even realizing that he wore glasses when he worked. Not that it mattered. She'd known all the important things in the first five minutes and tried to put them out of her mind ever since. She wasn't having much luck; that's why all the fresh air and sunshine didn't help.

Deke's next words confirmed it. "I think you should have spent your time resting. The way you look, you could haunt houses on your day off. What's the trouble—something bothering you?"

She could have told him that if he changed that to "someone," he might have the answer. She settled for saying, "The television reception here is terrible and it was too nice a day to stay inside. Did you see Obie?"

"A couple hours ago." He let the subject be changed reluctantly. "He sent you his best. The doctor says he can go back to the lodge with us tomorrow."

"Did the doctor say your back was all right?"

"How did you know about . . ." He caught himself and grinned slightly. "I should have recognized Jessica's hand in that maneuver."

"Actually, I heard Les paved the way."

"Not until he was given the word, I'll bet. Anyhow, the scratches are healing nicely." He looked at his watch. "Can you be dressed for dinner in twenty minutes? I made a reservation downstairs and Jessica's getting ready now. Les will meet us in the dining room."

As far as Melanie was concerned, another evening of making polite conversation across a dinner table seemed almost too much of an effort just then. But even as she hesitated, he moved toward her.

"What's the matter? Don't you feel well?" There was concern in his voice. "You haven't heard a thing I said."

"Of course I have." She managed to unlock her door and push it open, using it as a shield until she blinked away the sudden moisture in her eyes. "I was just wondering what to wear. Is this a dress-up occasion?"

"Damned if I know . . . what difference does it

148

make? Wear whatever you want." He turned then and went back to his door. "I'll pick you up."

"Don't bother." Her voice caught him as he started in his room. "I'll meet you at the table. That way, it won't matter if I'm late."

He shrugged. "Whatever you say," and closed the door behind him.

When she finished getting ready she took a last appraising look in the mirror. Her floor-length gown of nylon jersey was practical for packing but that's where the "sensible" adjectives stopped. The frosted mint shade brought out the golden highlights in her hair and made the most of her lightly tanned skin. The dress itself was deceptively simple in style with butter-fly capped sleeves and a slashed neckline on the bodice plus a softly flowing skirt that was pure whistle bait. Melanie wrinkled her nose derisively at her image but added a dollop of Patou's Moment Supreme for a final touch.

Her reception in the dining room was short but satisfying. Les, looking unusually somber in a navy blue blazer, muttered "Mamma mia!" in such a fervent tone that Melanie was almost embarrassed.

"Anyone would think you'd missed me," she told him to bridge the moment.

"Did we miss you?" His arms went out in an extravagant gesture. "Is the Archbishop of Canterbury a practicing member of the faith? Does Jack Nicklaus play golf? Did Casanova sleep on his . . ."

Deke cleared his throat hastily to cover the rest of that sentence and glared across at him.

Les grinned unrepentently. "I think you can safely say that we missed you," he concluded as he held her chair.

Jessica, looking fabulous herself in a ruffled red lace dress, winked, and added, "Deke said you'd be along. Will you have champagne with us?"

"Thank you. I'd like that." Melanie sat down across the round table.

Deke's glance was still on her. Melanie thought his face looked weary although it might have been the oddly formal effect of his dark gray suit and crisp white shirt.

"Deke . . . aren't you going to flag the waiter for another glass?" Jessica finally asked.

He made a wry grimace. "There's no need. He's on his way." He jerked his head toward the end of the room, as he added to Melanie, "Your arrival didn't go unnoticed."

She flushed and resisted an urge to pull her deep V-shaped neckline together. Instead she took a deep breath and said, "This is a beautiful room. It's nice to see a place at the ocean where the decorators haven't gone overboard with seagull pictures, shells, and driftwood."

"Or been seduced by the salesman who sells shag carpets," Jessica agreed.

"Even that's not as bad as the motel rooms around the country that look like a hangover from the Spanish Inquisition."

The other woman nodded. "Full of Tiffany-shaded

lamps with big gold chains cinching them to the wall. As if anybody would want to steal them."

"They must have some attraction," Deke said. "But it can't be illumination. The lights are so dim in those places that you have to grope your way to bed—let alone trying to read after you've gotten there." He paused as a waiter arrived to pour champagne for Melanie, before picking up his glass. "What shall we drink to—the here and now?"

"Fair enough," Les said. "The here and now. Let tomorrow look out for itself."

Melanie took a sip with the rest and then settled back in her chair, letting her glance roam around the room. She admired the cheerful red carpet and the walnut paneling on three sides of the room. At the ocean side, gleaming white cloths covered the tables in front of floor-to-ceiling windows which provided a fabulous view over the Pacific. There was a baby grand at the end of the room with a pianist offering a pleasant yet unobtrusive musical background.

Deke was following her glance. "They have dancing a little later. The pianist gives way to a combo but they're low-key, too."

"Then I approve," she told him and dropped her eyes to the glass she held between her fingers.

"I do, too," Jessica said. "In fact, this hotel gives the lodge a run for its money. If they only had decent television down here—I tried to watch a program while I was dressing and the reception was terrible."

"Why bother to turn it on?" Deke asked idly.

"With only a weekly newspaper, you have to do

something. And you should hear the local radio stations! They were featuring chicken mash and baby ducks on a swap program the last time I was here."

"I think that sounds pretty refreshing," Melanie observed, "compared to the news programs I hear at home."

"I agree with you," Deke put in. "It's not all sweetness and light, though, even in this part of the world." He turned to Les. "I never heard the follow-up on that assault case. You know the one I mean," he persisted when the other man looked blank. "The police had been holding him on suspicion."

"Oh, the one connected with the bank robbery."

"Which bank robbery are you talking about?" Jessica wanted to know.

"It wasn't far from here," Deke explained. "A couple of men made off with some cash and bearer bonds plus wounding a guard in the process."

"So much for your wilderness isolation," Jessica scoffed. "Probably two of the locals got tired of listening to the weather reports and the tide conditions."

"That isn't funny." Les gave her a hard look. "People here are the same as anywhere else."

She patted his arm on the table next to her. "Sweetie, you don't have to make noises like the local Chamber of Commerce. They'll probably find out that it was done by some bank robbers from Los Angeles who came up here and had to pay for a weekend of fishing."

Les grinned back at her before taking a menu from the hovering maître d'. "Frankly, I'd rather talk about food than bank robberies. Of course, I *worked* today, which is more than some people can say."

"Deke and I were working, too," Jessica replied, diverted. "So you needn't sound smug."

"That makes Melanie the only lounge lizard," Les said, lowering his menu to look at her. "You should have gone over to the clinic to visit Dad. He would have been glad to see you."

"I didn't want to be in the way. I understand he's going back to the lodge tomorrow."

"That's the plan," Deke cut in although he kept his glance on the leather-covered menu in his hands. "Jessica heads back to California, so we'll take her out to the airport and pick up Obie at the clinic on our way back to the boat. Do you have the whole day off?" he asked Les as an afterthought.

The other nodded. "The way it stands now. Is anybody else having steak or am I the only one?"

"I'd rather have salmon," Jessica said.

"Crab au gratin, please," Melanie said in response to Deke's inquisitive look.

He nodded and set about the serious business of ordering their meal.

"More calories," Jessica murmured to Melanie while he was busy with it. "So much for my diet. But then I might as well get fat . . . there's nothing else left to do." She went on to explain in an undertone. "So far I haven't had any luck . . . even red lace hasn't helped."

"I can't believe it. It's a gorgeous gown," Melanie said truthfully.

Jessica selected a stalk of celery from the relish dish and salted it. "Well, the outfit isn't a total loss. I know an accountant in San Francisco who has low sales resistance. My type exactly."

"You might find out if he has a friend."

"What are you two huddling about?" Deke asked suspiciously once the maître d' disappeared with the order.

"The importance of finding a good accountant," Jessica said.

"And keeping him," Melanie added firmly.

"I didn't know you were interested in accounting," Deke sounded puzzled as he stared at her across the table.

"Just certain aspects of the subject," Jessica said, answering for her. "Every woman is. It's a talent we're born with." She thrust the relish dish at him. "I can recommend the celery."

After that, dinner went smoothly. The three-piece combo replaced the pianist by the time they reached dessert. Neither Deke nor Les seemed anxious to reach the dance floor and they were on their second cup of coffee before Jessica gave Melanie a resigned look.

"There's no use being subtle," she said. "Look, you two," she turned to the men, "the baseball season will still be around even if you take your minds off it for a while. That music is going to waste."

Deke smiled as he said to Les. "There might be a chance for us if they weren't playing a fox trot."

"Speak for yourself." Les pushed back his chair and

beckoned to Melanie. "You have to make allowances for people like Deke who never get out of the woods. I've been tapping my foot for the last fifteen minutes."

She went into his arms at the edge of the dance floor. "You're good," she said before they'd gone more than a few feet. "Why didn't you say something before this?"

"I was afraid to." He pushed back a little so he could look down at her. "Since Women's Lib came in— I'm not sure who asks who. Or is it whom?"

She laughed and let him pull her close again. They danced effortlessly through some show tunes and stayed on the floor as the combo segued into a group of current hits. From the corner of her eye, Melanie saw Deke lead Jessica on to the floor during the second set. By then, many of the dinner patrons were dancing but she noticed that, for a man who spent most of his time on a rugged mountainside, Deke was perfectly at ease in his present surroundings.

When the music stopped the next time, he and Jessica were beside them on the dance floor. The lead musician announced briefly, "a Cole Porter medley . . . by request."

There was a moment of hesitation and then Jessica said to Les, "This must be our turn."

He reached for her hand. "My pleasure. C'mon, I like that beat."

Deke and Melanie watched them disappear back into the throng. Then, almost reluctantly, he put his arm around her waist. There was a good six inches between them as they started circling the floor.

"You dance very well," he said eventually, "but with all your talents, that's not surprising, is it?"

Melanie closed her eyes and mentally counted to ten. Apparently hostilities were still the order of the day. "*Si vis pacem, para bellum,*" she murmured to give herself courage, deciding to follow the Roman axiom of "If you want peace, prepare for war."

"I beg your pardon?" He peered down at her.

"I was deciding when to step on your foot."

His lips twitched. "I have the feeling that I should apologize again. Look at me, will you?"

Then, as her clear hazel eyes stared steadily up at him, he murmured something violent under his breath, dropping his hand to pull her snug against him as they danced on.

When they came abreast of the musicians, the overhead lights were suddenly dimmed and the clarinetist was spotlighted for a solo interlude. He gave the familiar melody of "Smoke Gets in Your Eyes" a haunting tempo that was almost sensual in its appeal. The dancers remained in place, listening. Deke's arm tightened to draw Melanie even closer and she found her head fitting neatly against his shoulder as if it belonged there.

The music went on but she couldn't have told for how long; she was only aware of the man who was holding her and the rare feeling between them. There was no need to ask if Deke felt the same way; it was evident in his protective clasp and in his breathing as he brushed her temple with his cheek—as if he needed reassurance as much as she did.

There was a moment of quiet on the dance floor when the music stopped. Then spontaneous applause broke out. The clarinetist nodded his thanks while the room lights came up and the group went on to a medley of Glenn Miller favorites.

Melanie blinked as if she'd been in a deep sleep and only just surfaced. Deke's expression indicated he was in the same mood.

"Let's get out of here," he said, running a finger around his collar. "I could use some fresh air. There's sort of a deck off the lobby." He took her arm and propelled her ahead of him through a side entrance to the dining room.

"But Jessica . . . and Les . . . what will they think?"

"That we went out to get some air." His eyes were amused as he glanced down at her but he slowed his pace. "Sorry, I didn't mean to make you run."

"That's all right." She paused for him to open a glass door and then walked ahead of him onto a shadowed deck overlooking the deserted beach. They wandered slowly over to the waist-high wooden balcony and leaned against it, listening to the subdued roar of the breakers.

"We must be the only ones with this idea," she said, more to make conversation than anything else. Then, when he didn't answer, she went on almost desperately, "The fresh air does feel good."

He accorded that remark the silence it deserved, too, and frowned as he stared over the railing. For all his irritation, he seemed different, Melanie thought. If she hadn't known better, she would have thought he was uneasy—unsure about something.

Deke cleared his throat and turned to her, "There's something I want to say to you. Maybe this isn't the best time but there's no use postponing it any longer." He hesitated again as if searching for the exact words he wanted.

A sense of foreboding knifed through Melanie. He was going to ask her to leave Tukwila. In the nicest possible way, he was going to explain that it would be better all around if she simply made herself scarce.

As Deke opened his mouth to continue, she cut in quickly. "I have something to tell you, too. This seems to be a night for confessions."

He looked puzzled. "I wouldn't exactly call it that."

"All right," her smile was brilliant as it flicked over him, "call it what you will. At any rate, I'll have to admit you're right—"

"What in the devil are you talking about?"

"You've heard the story before. Woman from the city falls in love with this wilderness country and takes to the Rogue for a vacation. Man who lives there takes to the hills in defense. Woman finally takes powder. Then they both live peacefully ever after. I think it's called the 'Great Farewell Scene.'"

"Why don't you stop being clever." There was a hint of steel in his voice.

"Okay." She kept her glance on the quiet beach in front of her. "I'm trying to tell you that I have to move on. I called my boss earlier today and he thought I'd loafed long enough." The lies came easily to her lips just as if she made a habit of them. "No more rest cure—it's back to the grindstone." If she embroidered the truth any more, Deke would be suspicious. Although it was difficult to tell what he thought as he stood in the shadows. "Of course, I can wait until Obie's settled in and things are back to normal at the lodge."

"Before you move on." It was a flat statement.

"Well, yes—if you put it that way." He needn't sound so ominous, Melanie decided. She'd done him a favor; once he thought it over, he'd realize it. Or maybe he did now but knew it wasn't polite to send up skyrockets.

"I see." He turned to stare with her at the breakers on the shoreline, which looked like ribbons of silver against the dark sand. His voice was quiet when he spoke again, "In that case, there's nothing else to say, is there?"

"I suppose not." She shivered as a breeze brushed her bare arms.

Deke must have caught the movement. "We'd better go back in or you'll get chilled. You should have said something earlier," he added sternly as he motioned for her to precede him.

"It doesn't matter. Deke, I hate to . . ." She bit her lip as she searched for words. It wouldn't hurt to give him an inkling of how she felt in case she'd gotten things wrong. He didn't *look* as if he felt overjoyed at her decision.

"Go ahead," he prompted, "you started to say . . ."

Before Melanie could speak they heard the sound

of a door opening behind them and looked around to see Jessica framed in the opening.

She smiled as she came toward them, pulling a stole around her shoulders. "Les and I wondered if you'd deserted us forever, so I decided to come hunting. Am I interrupting anything?"

"No, of course not." Deke's voice didn't give any indication of his feelings. "We were just about to come back and join you." He turned to Melanie, adding, "You'd better go on inside; that wind is getting stronger all the time."

She nodded, wishing they could have had another minute alone and then deciding that there was no use fighting fate. At least this way, she could leave with her pride still intact. "I'll see if I can find Les."

"You won't have to look far. I left him by the television set in the lobby," Jessica said carelessly over her shoulder as she moved to stand beside Deke at the railing. "Are those the lights of a ship out there?"

"Probably." He was still watching Melanie. "We'll start back to the lodge in the middle of the morning so you won't have to set your alarm. Obie needs to be discharged by his doctor before he can leave the clinic."

"And I don't want to get to the airport too early," Jessica reminded him. "They converted that waiting room from a barn, and since the cows didn't need any heat, they figured passengers wouldn't want it either."

Melanie didn't wait to hear more. "I'll be going along then. G'night." She slipped through the door before either of them had a chance to reply and slowed her pace as she turned toward the lobby. She wasn't anxious to find Les, but good manners demanded that she say "Good night" to him before she disappeared in her room.

As Jessica had said, he was in a semicircle of people watching the only television set in the lobby. The program was a newscast from Portland with a local commentator discussing recent developments on the Oregon crime scene. A picture of a bearded man was flashed on the screen as the newscaster reported, "John O'Brien, a thirty-year-old unemployed laborer, was the man Gold Beach authorities had in for questioning again today after witnesses placed him at the scene where the sensational bank robbery took place. Shortly after his initial release a few days ago, O'Brien was severely beaten in Gold Beach by a still-unidentified assailant. Today, the man was taken back into custody by the local police although it is not known if a formal charge has been lodged against him."

Melanie decided that she didn't want to hear any more of the program. "Les," she plucked at his sleeve to get his attention. "I won't interrupt," she whispered when he looked around, frowning. "I just wanted to say that I'll see you in the morning."

Behind them, the newscast was abruptly interrupted by an ad for a deodorant that sent most of the listeners scattering.

"You're not interrupting anything," Les said, moving with her toward an old-fashioned stairway which led up from the lobby to the guest rooms in the main part of the hotel. "I'll walk you to your room. I can cut through to the parking lot afterwards."

"Are you leaving, too?" Melanie asked politely as they went up the carpeted treads. "I thought I was the only one who was tired. The television is so awful that I thought I'd try to find some music on the radio," she went on, wondering why she was chattering with such determination when Les was obviously thinking of something else. "Deke said that we'll be leaving in the middle of the morning."

"I may have to leave before that." Les paused on the stair landing next to a long window overlooking the deck and the ocean. "I meant to tell Deke at dinner. My boss wants me to put in some extra hours tomorrow."

"But how will we get back to Tukwila?"

"That's no problem. There's an excursion boat that leaves in the middle of the morning. You can make arrangements to have them stop at the lodge."

"I see." Melanie's forehead wrinkled as she tried to think. "Won't you be going upriver past the lodge?"

"Probably." He was staring through the window beside him. "But I'll be leaving right after it gets light."

"Then you'd better tell Deke."

He grinned suddenly and shook his head. "I'll leave a note at the desk. This is no time to interrupt the man." He jerked his chin toward the glass.

Melanie moved over to look down. She was just in time to see two familiar figures merge in a shadowed corner of the deck. Jessica smiled radiantly up at Deke as her arms went around his neck and his hands found her waist. It didn't take any imagination to realize what would happen next. Melanie stepped back

rom the window, keeping her glance averted. "You're
ight. This is no time to interrupt."

"I'll go back down to the desk now. See you, honey."
His tone was casual.

"Les . . . just a minute." He was halfway down the
tairs when her call caught him. "Could I go with you
n the morning?" she begged. "I just found out today
:hat I have to go back home and the extra time at the
lodge would help for my packing."

Les wasn't enthusiastic. "When I say early, that's
what I mean," he told her tersely. "There won't be
time for more than coffee. We should be on the river
by six. Can you manage that?"

"I'll be ready." Her fingers were white with tension
as she gripped the stair railing. "Will you phone my
room or shall I meet you in the lobby?"

"Make it down here at five thirty. I'll have my
car," he said.

Melanie had plenty of time during that long sleep-
less night to go over her decision, but she was never
in any doubt that she'd made the proper one. The
less time she spent in Deke's company from now on,
the better it would be. That last view of him as he
held Jessica in his arms just confirmed what she'd sus-
pected all along. He was as easily swayed by an attractive woman as any other man, provided the surroundings were right. Melanie smiled grimly as she thought
about it. The moral of that story was never to under-
estimate the effects of a red lace dress.

She was packed and waiting in the deserted lobby
when Les drove up in the early light. He looked almost

as weary as she did when he muttered "G'morning" and threw her bag on the rear seat. Then, getting back behind the wheel, he stepped on the accelerator as soon as she slid in beside him.

A half hour later, Melanie was watching him cast off the line at the stern of the mail boat before they headed for the middle of the Rogue.

There was a mournful cry from overhead, and she looked up to see the dark form of a fish hawk banking in a huge arc against the pale early morning sky. How appropriate, she thought bitterly, for a final touch.

Even back in Greek times, the cry of a fish hawk was an ominous signal . . . a warning of evil or impending doom. And from the way things were going, this one was certainly to be congratulated on his timing!

Chapter Eight

Les stopped twice to make deliveries on his way up the Rogue, but it was still early when he pulled in to the dock at Tukwila. By then, Melanie had enough experience to be ready with the bow line as soon as the boat was nudged to the float while Les tied up at the stern.

"Too bad you're not going to be around longer," he commented, reaching back to get her overnight bag before they started walking to the lodge. "You could be a handy crew for a man to have around."

"I'll remember that if I need a job, but I'd rather be at the wheel."

"So you could put the coals to it?" His tired face creased in a grin. "If I'd known I was encouraging competition, I'd have dumped you overboard in the last riffle."

"Exactly why I didn't say anything." They trudged up the sandy bank to the Tukwila stairs. "Are you going back downriver soon?"

"Hard to say," he evaded. "I have some things to do first. You're not planning on pulling out today, are you?"

"Not if it means leaving your father in the lurch. On the other hand, if he's back to normal, there's no point in my waiting around. Martha's a real treasure —you were lucky there."

"She's okay, but what's your hurry? Oh, I know what you said," he added, "but I gather there's more to it than that. Did Deke ruffle your feathers last night?"

"Of course not. He was a perfect gentleman. And you needn't grin like an idiot—that wasn't the trouble either."

"With women, it's hard to tell."

She ignored that. "I simply have to get back home. But I'll check with Martha before I make any firm plans."

"Okay. Sorry I can't be more help. I'll put your bag in your room. Tell Martha I'll be in touch later, will you? There are some more deliveries to be made upstream."

"All right." Melanie watched him take the stairs two-at-a-time before she turned and walked across the cement deck of the lodge. Automatically she checked the moisture of the soil under the petunias as she went by and nodded approvingly. Martha had evidently been working outside as well.

Alfie came skidding into the sitting room as soon as he heard her steps.

"Hey, take it easy," Melanie reproved him, almost losing her balance as he put his big paws on her chest and washed her chin. "You're too big!"

"That's what I keep telling him," Martha said

from the kitchen doorway, "but he doesn't pay any attention."

"You're spoiled, Alfie," Melanie scolded and then proceeded to compound the felony as she rumpled the hair on his long nose and scratched behind his ears.

"Where is everybody?" Martha took another step into the room. "Didn't Obie come?"

"He'll be here later. I begged a ride with Les. He had to work an extra shift and it was too early for his father to leave the clinic."

"I can't think why you wanted to get up so early when you had a chance to sleep in." The housekeeper put her hands on her hips as she surveyed Melanie. "Seems to me that you could have used the rest. I don't think the beach helped at all. You looked better before you left."

"That's what comes from dancing half the night," Melanie said glibly, wishing she could tell the truth for a change. "I got the things on your list, though. They'll come on the second shift."

"Deke and Obie being the second shift, I gather." Martha was still staring at her.

"That's right." Melanie made her tone bright as she wandered over to the fish tank. "Is it feeding time again?" She looked over her shoulder and, as Martha nodded, reached down for a can of squid flakes. "You wouldn't think fish would need so many meals, would you?"

Martha wasn't led astray. "If Deke and Obie are coming later, why didn't you join them?"

"Because I'm going to have to leave Tukwila sooner

that I thought. I told Deke last night." Melanie kept her attention on the fish tank as she scattered dry food on the water. When there was no response to her announcement, she glanced reluctantly over her shoulder.

Martha's gaze was understanding. "I see," she said finally. Then, with a return to briskness, "I'll bet you didn't have a bite of breakfast."

"We swallowed some coffee on the dock."

The older woman's sniff showed what she thought of that. "I'll put on some bacon. If I know Les, he'll be routing through the refrigerator any time."

"He said that he had some deliveries to make."

"Maybe—but I'll bet that breakfast is the first thing on his list." A crash from the kitchen made her smile and start toward the door. "I'd better get in there or he'll drop every egg I have. Breakfast'll be on the table in ten minutes."

"All right, thanks." Melanie could see the sense in Martha's remark. Things might look brighter after something to eat. If she borrowed the truck to drive to Canfield later and hitched a ride from there she probably wouldn't have a chance for lunch. Not if she made her way back to the beach today.

Breakfast didn't hold her up materially. Martha seemed to understand that neither she nor Les was in a talkative mood. The bacon omelet was delicious and the toast was hot, but Melanie found it an effort to get the food down. When she'd managed most of it, she excused herself on the pretext of packing, leaving

Les to pour his second cup of coffee and fend off any more of the housekeeper's questions.

Packing in her room didn't take long either. After it was finished, Melanie stripped the bed and remade it with fresh linen and then went on to thoroughly clean the room. When it was as spotless as she could make it, she tucked a small package under her arm and let herself out into the hall. There was still time to go by the greenhouse for some unfinished business before she left the lodge.

A few minutes later, Martha found her there, hammering on the wooden frame. "I thought I heard you. What's going on?"

Melanie gestured toward the small wooden plaque she'd just mounted above some geraniums. It showed an unlikely flower and the motto "Bloom where you are planted." "Positive thought," she told Martha. "It's my going-away present."

Martha's severe mouth twitched. "Even if the geraniums don't get the word, Obie'll like it. So will Deke."

"Why would he care?"

"It's his greenhouse. He owns this whole place. I thought you knew."

Melanie paused in the middle of replacing the hammer on a potting shelf. "No, nobody told me," she said finally in a level tone.

"You didn't ask. It's no secret but he doesn't noise it around."

"He certainly doesn't. No wonder he was annoyed when Obie went over his head and hired me."

"Was he unhappy about that? S'funny—it doesn't

sound like Deke. He's always left the hiring and firing to Obie." Her smile was wintry. "But then, he's never had a household help that looked like you."

"With Jessica around, he wasn't missing anything."

"So that's the trouble." She pointed toward the proverb over the geraniums. "That sign could apply to most any living thing. Maybe Deke didn't think you'd survive transplanting. Couldn't weather this kind of life."

Melanie shook her head sorrowfully, intent on setting the record straight. "He didn't even give me a chance to try."

Martha would have answered but a glimpse of Melanie's disconsolate face kept her from saying more. She followed the younger woman on to the deck and stood beside her looking over the river.

Some of the mist that shrouded the oceanfront earlier in the morning still lingered over the Rogue. The sun's rays were dimmed by the moist air but a breeze bent the leaves on the madrona tree at the edge of the lodge patio and showed that another warm summer day was in the offing.

"When I leave I'm going to miss every inch of this lovely place," Melanie said. "I can see why Alfie keeps coming back."

Martha made a worried grimace. "That reminds me —was there anybody out here on the deck when you came down?"

"I don't think so but I didn't pay much attention. Les could have been down on the dock."

"Not Les." Martha gestured impatiently. "He left

a while back. I'm talking about the dog. That fool hound sneaked out to follow Les when I had my back turned. I thought he'd come back as soon as the boat was out of sight but I haven't seen him since." She bit her lip and continued worriedly, "I wouldn't think about it except that his ear is giving him trouble again. The vet prescribed an antibiotic cream to put on it but it has to be applied on schedule. Otherwise it doesn't do any good."

"Then I'd better go and look for him," Melanie said.

For the first time, Martha seemed to take in the other's neat sailcloth blazer and skirt. "But you're all dressed up," she said. "When you talked about moving on, surely you didn't mean today?"

"I was thinking about it," Melanie hedged, "but it wasn't definite." The way things were, she couldn't leave Martha until Alfie was safely home again. With any luck, she might still get downriver later on. Another thought struck her. "Maybe Alfie decided to have breakfast at Canfield."

"He wasn't headed toward Canfield the last time I saw him," Martha insisted stubbornly. "He was at Les's heels when he went down to the boat."

"Perhaps Alfie hitched a ride with him."

"I don't think so. Les didn't plan to stop here on the way downstream. He didn't say why." The older woman sounded aggrieved. "In fact, he hardly opened his mouth after he finished eating 'cept to say he had some business to look after."

Martha was having trouble extracting information from either of them, Melanie decided, feeling a sudden surge of sympathy for her. She put a comforting arm around the housekeeper's thin shoulders. "I'll go whistle for Alfie—he can't be too far away."

"That's a lot of foolishness. He could be halfway to California by now if he'd a mind to. I'm just hoping he had other ideas. Like the beef bone I'm saving for his dinner. His nose was on the draining board a half dozen times this morning trying to reach it."

"Then I doubt very much if he picked this day to leave home. I'll probably find him smelling the flowers or sleeping by the road like the other time."

"But you can't go hunting for him in that outfit."

"Why not? It's washable. And these are walking shoes." Melanie's sudden smile illuminated her face. "The clerk promised they were. If I come back limping, I'll demand a refund. Besides, I don't want to take time to change clothes again."

"Well, if you say so."

"I do." Melanie dropped a quick kiss on Martha's cheek and headed for the lodge door. "Keep the coffee pot on."

"Don't *you* get lost . . ."

"I won't. This time I'm not leaving the trail."

"I'll remember," Martha called after her. "But watch where you're going."

Melanie cast an envious look toward the truck parked in the drive as she set out. It would be easier to drive but not as practical. This way she could hear if the Afghan were cavorting through the under-growth nearby. It also gave her a chance to call and whistle to him which she couldn't do in the truck unless she stopped every fifty feet.

The expanse of isolated countryside which surrounded her as soon as the road passed the border of Tukwila property still made her marvel. A towering grove of fir trees grew thick along the track, cutting the sunlight into bright bits and pieces as it tried to penetrate the foliage. Melanie reached down to button her blazer as she passed through a shaded patch and wondered if she should have brought a heavier jacket after all. As she lingered, she cupped her hands and shouted, "Alfie! Alfie . . . come here!" The silence that followed her ringing cries was broken only by the rustle of the wind in the trees overhead. Alfie had evidently decided to explore farther afield.

"Idiot dog!" she thought as she started on again. Knowing Alfie's sense of the dramatic, he probably would enjoy every stolen moment before he was collared and led, unprotesting, back to his juicy bone in the kitchen. The only aftermath to his escapade would be a long relaxing nap in front of the fireplace.

She walked on steadily after that, calling at intervals and whistling but without any response from an erring Afghan hound. As she approached the rocks where she'd been marooned before, she frowned and checked her watch. If she hadn't any luck by the time she reached the mine entrance, she'd turn back toward the lodge.

This time the pine needles alongside the rutted track were smooth and happily unoccupied. The rattler she'd encountered the other day had moved on to better things, and Melanie stayed close to the high crown of the track to make sure she didn't disturb any of his friends or acquaintances.

A slight noise from beyond the rocks at the bend of the road made her pull up. She opened her lips to call "Alfie!" and then an unexpected measure of caution made her close them again. Alfie moved in an aura of rustling leaves and small excited barks; this was the sound of loose rock disturbed by heavier feet. Even as she listened, the sound was repeated but it came from farther away this time. Down toward the river, she thought, remembering that she'd made a similar disturbance exploring the loose shale on her ledge before Deke rescued her.

Even that fleeting thought of Deke made her move instinctively toward the bank where she'd been marooned. Then she stopped as logic took over; Deke couldn't have come searching for her now. She would have heard the noise of his boat along the river. This disturbance was more apt to be a hiker examining the deserted mine shaft—or one of the river rafters detouring to explore the river trail.

Melanie walked quietly back to the road and started following the track again. Once it reached the bend by the rock, she'd be able to see the mine shaft herself. If the old claim were deserted, then she'd check the river below from the top of the bank. Probably whoever it was would be well away by then, she told herself.

The bare grassy area next to the rocks let the sun blaze down and the warmth felt good. Melanie hugged her arms over her breast to quell a sudden shiver. Nerves! she told herself scornfully—which was ridiculous when she thought about it. A quick check of the mine and she'd be on her way. Probably Alfie had wandered back to Tukwila ages ago and would be waiting on the steps of the lodge to greet her.

But that vision left her thoughts as soon as she passed around the granite outcropping to her left. The gold mine loomed black and empty but it was the bulky canvas bag bound with nylon rope on the ground in front of the shaft that caught her attention. Even as she stared at it, a hummingbird darted from the shelter of some salal and hovered over it, as if he wondered what it was doing there, too. Then he moved off in his erratic lurching flight, leaving Melanie in sole possession of the territory.

For a half minute her curiosity battled with caution until the latter capitulated. She moved from her rock cover and went over to kneel beside the bag. It was covered with dirt but the grime brushed off easily and the canvas underneath her fingers looked strong and new.

There was some printing near the stained bottom of the pouch. Melanie pushed the bag on its side so she could try to figure out what it said. "Property of . . ." she read aloud and then brushed at the dirt impatiently to clear the next line.

". . . the United States Federal Reserve Bank," Les finished from behind her.

Melanie let out a startled shriek, staggering as she whirled and tried to stand up. "You scared me out of five years' growth," she told him hotly. "Did you have to sneak up on me like that?"

"If you hadn't been so damned curious about that bag, you would have heard me before this. It was quite a shock for me, too."

She stared at his tense figure. "Then it was you I heard before. I thought whoever it was had gone back down to the river."

"Don't ever try for a tracking job," he advised. "You'd never make it."

"Well, you don't have to be such a grouch," she complained, as her panic began to subside. "There's no reason to be unpleasant."

"Unpleasant! My God!" Les rubbed a grimy hand over the stubble on his chin, his expression bleak as he surveyed her. "You talk like this is some damned tea party. If you'd kept your nose out of things, you'd have been a lot better off." He came nearer and kicked disconsolately at the bag by her feet. "But I can't take any more chances—this time I need a head start."

She stared back at him in bewilderment. "I *still* don't know what all this is about. Martha sent me out to look for Alfie."

Les gave a snort of laughter. "That fool dog! I left him chewing a bone under that tree down by the dock."

"You mean I've spent all this time for nothing! Oh, damn!" Melanie struck her forehead with the heel of her palm in disgust. "Well, if your boat's nearby, maybe I can hitch another ride back to Tukwila with you." She was trying to ignore his stony face, but her glance flicked down to that canvas bag and then moved hastily back up again.

That was all Les needed. "I didn't think you'd forgotten it. Why don't you go ahead and say what's on your mind. Like—what's a bag from the Federal Reserve doing here?"

"I'd be pretty slow if I couldn't figure that one out," Melanie admitted. "People have been talking about a bank robbery every since I got here. It was in the newspaper the day I arrived." She went on carefully, spacing her words. "I'm wondering now what other cargo you were carrying that day you brought me to the lodge."

He reached in his shirt pocket for a cigarette and lit it without taking his eyes from her face. "Don't let your imagination run away with you. I've always believed in taking care of first things first. You were the most valuable cargo on that run."

"Then this"—Melanie nudged the canvas satchel with the toe of her shoe—"had already been stowed away in the mine shaft." She gave a mirthless smile. "And practically the first thing I did when I settled at Tukwila was talk about exploring up here."

"Yeah, I remember very well." He drew in on his cigarette and blew the smoke out in a cloud over her head. "So I had to take steps to discourage you." When she still looked puzzled, he went on, "The broken railing on your balcony."

She drew in her breath sharply. "*You* were the one."

He nodded and continued in a callous tone. "Nothing happened to you. The worst would have been some scratches from the shrubbery. But then you didn't take the hint and I had to try again. I followed you on the trail that day when you went over the bank. I had to get away afterwards—I wasn't supposed to be here."

"Your father . . . " she tried again. "He didn't know . . . "

Les deliberately dropped his cigarette on a rock and ground it viciously under his heel. "Not until the day you arrived."

Melanie's cheeks paled as she thought about it. "That's what caused his attack . . . why he changed so suddenly . . . it was the headline in the paper."

"Hell! If he'd been halfway reasonable about money, I wouldn't have gotten involved with the other guy in the first place. When I wanted to go back to school, Dad said no more handouts from him. I had to work for a living the way he did. He got me this part-time job on the river. With my paycheck, I'd have gray hair and a face like a prune before I could save anything." He went on bitterly, "If only that damned cop hadn't connected O'Brien with the robbery."

"O'Brien?"

"The guy they were talking about on that newscast at the hotel. The suspect they took back into custody."

"But he'd been beaten," she argued, trying to remember what she'd heard. "Wait a minute . . . " Her lips parted in horror. "Oh, Les . . . you weren't involved in *that*?"

"My God! You sound just like my dad! What was I supposed to do?" The words came out in a torrent.

"Sit around while the creep cops a reduced plea by selling out? O'Brien only understands one kind of persuasion to keep his mouth shut."

"Then why are you moving the money today?"

"I didn't know they were going to take him back into custody. The damn liar told me they didn't have anything on him, but he threatened to blow the lid on me before he took the rap for the bank guard. I thought I had him convinced—but he won't last a hot minute if the feds put the heat on him." Les shook his head decisively. "I'm getting out and taking my share. With any luck, I'll be across the border before they get the truth out of him."

She watched him bend over and start to untie the rope around the canvas bag. "It won't do you any good to take bearer bonds. The numbers on them . . ."

". . . are hot. You're not telling me anything. But they can still be fenced abroad. Even with a discount, there'll be enough to set me up for life. I've got it all planned." He stood up then, dangling the rope in his hand. "Unfortunately, you don't fit in the plan."

Her eyes were on that length of dirty rope, swinging gently back and forth like an ominous pendulum. She cleared her throat with an effort. "What are you going to do with that?"

His twisted smile was almost gentle. "Not what you think. There's no reason for me to kill you. Just put you away for a while. By tomorrow when somebody goes far enough in that mine shaft to find you, I'll be long gone." His voice coarsened. "You're damned lucky there'll even be a tomorrow for you. All I'd have to do is shove you into the river here." He jerked his head toward the steep bank "There's enough current and white water down there to kill you in the first fifty feet."

Melanie nervously moistened her lips with the tip of her tongue, but she found herself without words. It was obvious that Les knew what he was talking about; she wouldn't last any time at all in the river. Unfortunately for her, his alternative was almost as terrifying. Even as she opened her mouth to protest, he caught her wrists and shoved them behind her. An instant later she felt the nylon cord jerked tight against her skin.

"That'll do the trick," Les muttered as he finished knotting the rope. He caught her by the shoulder and pushed her ahead of him back toward the mine entrance. "There's some more rope in here for your ankles. And if you've got a handkerchief, better tell me where it is. It'll make a better gag than anything I have handy."

She dug her heels in at that. "Oh, no, Les—please! I can't do you any harm once you get away—you don't have to gag me."

"Don't be a damned fool! Martha will send somebody looking when you don't show up at the lodge and I need time." He put a heavy hand on her shoulder to shove her forward again. "Don't waste your breath. This is the only way."

After that, Melanie didn't have a chance to protest further. He kept a tight grip on her inside the dark mine shaft where they had to stoop because of the overhead timber bracing. Farther back, rivulets of water could be heard trickling down the rough rock walls.

Les muttered with satisfaction when he found another length of rope in the shadows. "Come back to the light," he told her, "I want to make sure this holds."

Melanie blinked in the sunshine once they stood in the entrance again. The trees growing by the rocks at the bend of the road had never seemed greener or the sky above them a deeper blue. Then the tears in her eyes blurred the sharp outlines and all she could see was the deep orange of Les's nylon windbreaker as he bent to tie her ankles.

"Sit down," he ordered. "There's no point in making this tougher on yourself than you have to."

Melanie winced as the rope cut into her skin. Les took an extra hitch and then knotted the cord at the front. "So you can't play any games with your hands behind you," he told her with a smirk of satisfaction. "Now for the gag . . . "

"No!" She tried again to make him change his mind. "If I promise on my word of honor . . . "

His fingers grasped her arm painfully. "Be quiet!" he ordered as she tried to stifle a moan. "Do you hear it?"

"Hear what?" she asked, playing for time. There'd been the sound of a truck . . . she was sure of it . . . although now the silence had settled down over the forest again. "You must be imagining things."

Les muttered something profane under his breath and hauled her back to her feet. "Maybe . . . but I'm taking no chances. Get back there in the shadows." He hauled her along like a sack of grain, shoving her finally against the side of the shaft. "Stay there! I'm going back to look around."

Melanie's thoughts raced chaotically as she watched him move to the mine entrance and peer around it cautiously. If only she knew what was happening out there.

Les stared down the track for another minute and then grimaced with satisfaction as he stepped back in the tunnel. "Nothing," he reported. "I'm getting too damned edgy." He hauled a stained rag from his jacket pocket and started twisting it. "Let's get this over with."

A sharp whistle from outside cut into his words, followed by Deke's deep voice shouting, "Melanie! Can you hear me?"

She didn't even think of the consequences. His words hadn't died away before she was screaming back, "Deke! I'm here!" Her call was sliced off as Les, with a furious oath, caught her jaw with the edge of his hand and sent her reeling.

She must have lost consciousness after that. The next thing that made sense was a gradual awareness of throbbing pain. She struggled to raise her head from the filthy tunnel floor as she felt grit on her lips and in her mouth. There was some kind of movement by the tunnel entrance but her eyes wouldn't focus properly to identify it. She closed them again when nausea threatened and retched weakly. After the spasm passed, she took a deep breath and lifted her eyelids one more time.

That interval must have taken longer than she thought because all was quiet. She started toward the mine entrance with a crablike lurch which made her heart pound and sandpapered her clothes.

It took another minute and a half to reach her objective. By then her blouse was in ribbons and her arms were scratched and bleeding, but she could see immediately that the unconscious figure sprawled at the entrance to the mine tunnel was in far worse shape. Deke Brandt's eyes were closed and blood oozed from a frightening wound on the side of his head.

The jagged piece of granite with stained red edges which lay in front of his limp body was a grisly reminder of exactly how Les had made his escape.

Chapter Nine

It would have been a luxury to cry.

Just then, Melanie only wanted to lay her head on Deke's chest and give free rein to the tears which were streaming down her dirty cheeks.

But even as she would have yielded to the urge, a stronger instinct made her struggle to sit up and look around for help. This was not a time to collapse; not when Deke's very life depended on her. His truck must be parked somewhere nearby, she reasoned, trying to think coherently—but first she had to get out of her bonds. She managed to push up on her knees and look around—trying to find something with sharp edges to sever the ropes.

Her gaze again passed over the stained rock by Deke's head and she shuddered visibly, wondering that he hadn't been killed outright. Any sympathy she might have felt for Les had long since disappeared. Just then Deke was her only concern and he wouldn't survive unless she started functioning again. She was squirming toward a sharp-edged boulder by the mine entrance when Obie's sturdy figure came round the bend.

His horrified glance took in her plight and then moved on to Deke's unconscious form by the mine entrance. "Good God almighty!" he muttered and he broke into a run. "It's all right," he said as he reached Melanie and started to untie her. "Don't cry like that, girl, you'll be sick."

"I know . . . " She tried to hold back the sobs. "But don't bother with me. It's Deke who needs help."

He gave another hasty glance over his shoulder. "Another minute or so won't make much difference to him and it'll take two of us to carry him." He stripped the rope impatiently from her ankles and reached up to untie her hands. "Was it Les?"

Melanie's eyes were still drenched with tears. She nodded reluctantly, trying to keep her lips steady. Obie's face looked as painful as the skin on her scraped wrists and ankles just then. "He must have gotten away downriver in his boat," she said.

"Did he take that damned haul from the bank with him?"

She looked around dazedly. "I guess so. At least, the bag's gone." Her eyes met his. "He told you about it?"

"I found out for sure the day he brought you to the lodge. Before that, he'd just been threatening to pull off some damned caper. Les was always good at talking," Obie added bitterly as he freed her hands. "Move around—you'll feel better when the circulation gets going."

"I'll be all right. Please—go help Deke." A moment later, she was able to hobble across and join him where he bent over that still form. "Hasn't he come 'round at all?"

Obie's somber glance rose to meet hers and he shook his head. "He needs more help than we can give him. We'll have to get him out of here. The truck's just around the bend. I'll bring it as close as I can."

She caught his arm as he got up. "But, Obie, that road's in terrible condition . . . wouldn't it be better to bring a doctor here? Deke's in no shape to be moved."

"You think I don't know that, girl!" His tone was fierce. "But time's the most important thing. If we can get him back to Tukwila, I'll drive on to Canfield and radio for the Coast Guard helicopter at the beach. They can set down on that pasture behind the lodge and take Deke aboard. After that, they'll have him at the hospital in Gold Beach within fifteen minutes." His weathered face softened as he saw the tears running down her cheeks. "Deke deserves the best. Now, stick with him while I get that truck."

After that, she followed his orders without question. Between them, they were able to lift Deke's unconscious body into the back of the truck, sweeping aside the clutter and boxes of rock samples as they eased him onto the hard flooring. Melanie tried to cushion his head with her jacket.

"I'm afraid to raise him very much," she said worriedly to Obie. "With a head wound, it could be dangerous."

He nodded grimly. "I'll try and miss the potholes

but you'll have to watch over him. Make sure that he doesn't shift around and get in more trouble."

"All right." She wedged herself into place by Deke's shoulders, uncaring of her comfort. "Go ahead. I'll tell you if I need help."

When Obie slammed the back of the truck and went around to crawl in the driver's seat, she adjusted Deke's head so that one cheek was resting against her thigh and the other braced with the palm of her hand. As the truck moved off, she pushed her shoulder against the back of the driver's seat for balance.

Deke's features looked strangely young in repose. His lashes were dark crescents against a tightly drawn skin that had the color of a papyrus scroll. If only those lashes would lift—even for an instant—she thought with a surge of fierce longing. So I could tell him it's all right . . .

Her hand tightened protectively against his cheek as Obie drove over a section of washboard road and the truck lurched alarmingly. "It won't be much longer," she whispered to Deke, as she huddled over him. "Hang on, darling—don't give up." The last was murmured fervently as she grasped his hand and brought it up against her lips for comfort.

His eyelids didn't move, but just for an instant she thought there was a tremor of response in those lean fingers. She drew in her breath sharply and kept his hand against her lips for the rest of the way back to the lodge, as if willing him her strength as well as her prayers.

When they arrived at Tukwila, Obie gave a worried glance over his shoulder as he turned off the ignition. "No change?" He didn't wait for her response before he was going on. "Then let's not move him. I'll get the other truck in the garage and drive down to Canfield. With luck, there should be a 'copter here in forty-five minutes. I'll give them all the background over the radio. You stay here and take care of him—Martha can spell you."

"Oh, Obie . . . " She bit down hard on her lip to keep it steady. "Just go!"

"I know, girl." He lingered an instant longer to pat her shoulder. "It won't be long now."

Melanie wasn't aware of how fast the time passed after that. She did know that Martha waited with her, sitting quietly on the front seat after Melanie flatly refused to move from Deke's side. Eventually there was the noise of the helicopter overhead, but it wasn't until the crewman appeared at the back of the truck and arranged the basket stretcher that Martha was able to lead Melanie away.

There was a doctor, too, who materialized from somewhere and came up in the truck to bend over his patient. A little later as Deke was being transported toward the waiting 'copter, the doctor sought Melanie out on the front steps of the lodge. He took in her grief-stricken face and said something about "One patient was a great plenty," before leading her inside and administering a sedative.

She had only a dim recollection of Martha settling her in a familiar bedroom before the medication took hold and everything blurred into a gray nothingness.

It was noon the next day before she finally awakened from that drugged sleep. She opened her eyes to find Martha sliding a lunch tray onto a table near the bed.

"I want you to eat every bit of that food," she instructed Melanie, "because I plan to go down to the beach on the afternoon mail boat and find out how Deke is. I can't leave you alone here if you're not up to snuff."

Melanie sat up. "You'll be on that boat even if I have to put you there myself. You haven't heard any reports yet?"

Martha's expression softened. "The doctor said not to expect any news until today. Something about Deke's condition stabilizing. It's almost as easy for me to go down to the hospital as to wait here for a message. Besides, I'm worried about Obie—I thought he'd be back by now."

Melanie frowned, remembering Obie's look when he'd seen what Les had done. She moved over to take Martha by the shoulders and turn her toward the door. "Get your hat on—I don't want you to miss that boat. And don't worry if you can't get back tonight. I'll take care of things here."

"I hoped you'd feel that way." Martha lingered with her hand on the knob. "Alfie's asleep in the kitchen, he'll be company for you." She managed a bleak smile. "Keep your fingers crossed."

"They've been that way for hours. Give . . . everybody . . . my best."

Martha nodded and was gone.

But the next morning when the mail boat arrived, Martha's familiar figure wasn't sitting amidships. A grizzled boatman snubbed the craft up to the pier as efficiently as Les had done earlier and handed over a note "From Martha" with the rest of the lodge mail.

"*Deke's going to be okay,*" Martha had scrawled hastily, knowing what Melanie wanted to hear. "*The doctors say he is out of danger now and on the mend but it will take a while to recover from his concussion. Deke sent word for me to stick around Tukwila until he can get back next week. He doesn't know that Obie's here at the beach in Les's apartment waiting for news. I think I'd better stay nearby to make sure he eats regular and takes his pills. Can you hold things together at the lodge until I come back at the end of the week? That'll be before Deke returns so he won't need to worry. Send word by the boatman if this is okay.*"

Melanie looked up to find the mail-boat pilot watching her with outright curiosity. "Martha's arrangement will be fine," she told him.

"Okay, I'll let her know as soon as I get back to the beach." He turned to loosen the bow line. "We were damned glad to hear that Deke was going to be okay," he added. "Too bad Obie's troubles can't be cured in the hospital, too."

"He hasn't heard from Les?"

"Nary a word." He stepped back into the boat, gesturing for her to loosen the stern line. "This morning there was a report that some car went over a cliff just north of the California line. The State Patrol's still trying to get some information on the owner. I'll let you know tomorrow if there's anything new. Have a list ready if you want Martha to go shopping for you." He reached for the throttle and the boat roared off. Melanie automatically braced herself as the wake hit the wooden dock.

The news of Deke's recovery that she'd just received brought forth a flood of relief as powerful as the rooster tail raised by the departing jet boat, and Martha's request for her to stay at the lodge gave her time to pull herself together after the strain of the past days. As long as she was gone from Tukwila before Deke returned, nothing else mattered.

She reached over to pat Alfie's dusty nose as he galloped down from the deck to meet her. "We're on our own, my friend," she told him. "You'd better behave or no more cookies for breakfast. Sometime before Martha gets back, I'll give you a bath." As the Afghan cocked a suspicious head, she smiled and tugged his ear. "It's okay—you can combine it with fetching sticks from the river. I think, Alfie m'love, that we deserve a treat."

The next few days followed a deliberate pattern; mornings were spent in keeping the lodge spic and span and afternoons were devoted to a session beside the pool or frolicking with Alfie on the riverbank. When the summer sun lost its strength late in the day, they adjourned to the garden. Alfie eventually learned to restrict his cultivating efforts to the berry patch where he couldn't do much harm. After he finished excavating and Melanie finished hoeing, they went back to the lodge for an early dinner.

Bedtime was early, too, since that was the part of the day when Melanie's thoughts played traitor and dwelled on what might have been. On nights like that, she gave up trying to sleep and, instead, read the novels on her bedside table until sheer physical exhaustion took over.

Saturday morning dawned bright and clear. Melanie spent an extra hour polishing the furniture in the living room and even buffed the glass on the fish tank so that everything would be perfect when Martha arrived. She brought in fresh flowers from the cutting garden and warned Alfie sternly about muddy paws on beige carpets. After that, she ruined the lecture by scratching his chin and telling him it was time for a swim. However, once they'd finished, she was careful to see that he settled for his nap in a sunny spot on the deck while she made her way to her room for a more leisurely bath.

She turned on both taps full force and sprinkled some perfumed crystals in the water before stacking slacks and a clean blouse on the hamper. A quick glimpse in the mirror showed that she needed the restoration; her hair was tousled and her thigh-length hoppi-coat clung in wrinkled abandon to her wet swimsuit after cavorting with Alfie on the riverbank. She wrinkled her nose at her reflection and bent over to turn off the bath water when she heard a disturbance outside.

She tightened the belt on her robe and went through

the bedroom to see what was happening from her balcony, when she heard the roar of the mail boat on the river. Just then there was a knocking on her bedroom door.

Martha, of course. The noise of the bath water had cloaked her arrival. Melanie turned back to the middle of the room. "For heaven's sake—come in. I didn't hear you . . ."

The corridor door swung toward her and Deke's tall form in the opening made Melanie freeze in her tracks. From down by the dock, she heard Alfie's staccato barks blend with the commotion of the jet boat but they made no more impression than the golden bars of sunlight criss-crossing the rug at her feet. All her attention was centered on the man standing relaxed in front of her and when she breathed his name, she wasn't even aware that she'd spoken aloud.

He came in and closed the door behind him, leaning against it as his glance went over her. His voice sounded deep and full of laughter. "You were wearing that outfit once before. I think this is where I came in."

She stared back at him, still uncomprehending. "But you aren't supposed to be here. Martha said . . ."

" . . . exactly what I told her to." He didn't dwell on that. Instead he jerked his head toward the bathroom. "Go get dressed, will you."

The flush that suddenly covered half her body didn't contribute to Melanie's poise or self-possession. Anger at her total inadequacy to remain calm in a situation she had tried so hard to avoid made her stubborn. "I *am* dressed. There's a perfectly good swimsuit on under this coat."

"Don't argue. It's a damned fool thing for a man in a weakened condition to even be in the same neighborhood with you."

"I was just going to clean up when I heard your knock . . ." she admitted, deciding that she could use a few minutes to get her pulse rate back in order. "I won't be long . . . "

"Go ahead. I'll wait out here for you." He shoved his hands in the pockets of his cotton slacks. Aside from his face looking slightly thinner than usual, there was no evidence of his hospital stay.

Melanie wasn't aware of the concern on her face as she hesitated outside her bathroom door. "Deke—you're all right? Really all right?"

"I'm fine. Or at least, I plan to be," he added obscurely, "once things are threshed out."

His stern mouth relaxed when he said it and Melanie decided that maybe things weren't as bad as she feared. "I'll be out in a minute," she promised. And then, because she couldn't help herself, "Don't go away."

The bath that followed could probably have gone down in *The Guinness Book of Records* for its brevity. She stepped into the water and emerged, minutes later, to hastily dry herself with a convenient bath sheet. Slipping into her clothes was another maneuver that would have earned admiration from a quick-change artist. It wasn't until it came to combing her hair and applying a faint touch of lipstick that Melanie slowed her pace thoughtfully.

When she walked back into the bedroom, she was hoping that her yellow shantung blouse, which enhanced her tan so nicely, didn't reveal how hard her heart was beating under its fragile covering.

Deke was sitting on the edge of her bed, leafing through a book from the collection on her night table. He put it aside and stood up as she came toward him.

"Would you like some coffee?" she asked him politely, proud of her light tone. "I brought a thermos up after breakfast. It's here someplace." She turned toward the bureau, glad of an excuse to escape his brooding gaze. "There must be another cup around, too. Half a second and I'll rinse it."

"Forget the coffee. There's only one thing I came here for," he said, dispensing with her breathless chatter as if it didn't exist. "I've been going crazy this past week for fear you'd run out on me before I could tell you." His voice became more gentle as he saw the sudden stiffening of her back and the way her hands gripped the top of the bureau. "I love you, Melanie. I want to marry you—that is, if you'll have me." As she started to turn toward him, and he saw the emotion in her face, his tone went rough with longing. "Put that damned thermos down and come here. I've had about all of this a man can take."

Then she was in his arms and his lips were on hers as if he'd never let her go. Those first hungry kisses were everything that she'd dreamed about for so long—passion, need, and pure pleasure. The hands she felt caressing her were the skillful hands of an experienced lover, and she responded instinctively, relieved that she didn't have to hide her feelings any longer.

Sometime in the interval that followed, they gravitated to the edge of the bed and when Melanie finally surfaced after a kiss that left her weak and trembling, she pushed up on an elbow and stared at him with a shaky smile. "We'll have to stop this. Please, Deke darling, I mean it," she insisted as he merely grinned and reached for her again. "It's awful to try and remember I'm a lady when I'd so much rather forget it. At this rate, I'll need a psychiatrist or a hospital bed."

He laughed at that and sat up beside her, capturing her hand when she attempted to rearrange her blouse. "I know it'll be a damned lot safer if we move off this bed. How about that coffee you mentioned earlier?"

She nodded, grateful that he understood. "There's another cup in the cabinet in the bathroom," she told him and wasn't surprised that he merely nodded and went to find it. By the time he'd returned, she'd had time to run a comb through her hair and attain a semblance of normalcy despite the undercurrent of awareness and desire that passed between them.

Melanie dropped her eyes to the coffee she was pouring and tried for a lighter atmosphere. "What did you mean about telling Martha to keep me here? From the way you acted down at the ocean, I thought you couldn't wait to get rid of me." She handed him the cup of coffee and decided to be truthful. "I saw you with Jessica afterwards . . ."

Her revelation didn't appear to bother him. "I thought you might." He touched the end of her nose with a teasing finger and then moved to a safer distance by the balcony door. "Served you right. How in the hell did you think I felt? You'd just told me that you couldn't wait to leave—after keeping out of sight the whole afternoon. You were pretty convincing. I didn't know whether to strangle you right there or lure you into my hotel room and throw away the key."

Her eyes danced. "A fate worse than death . . ."

"Watch it, my love. That last part still sounds like a good idea."

"Don't tempt me." She put out her hand when he would have moved. "No, stay over there . . . for now anyway," she temporized weakly and saw his silent laughter. "Beast! Tell me about Jessica—and then I can forget it."

"I should hope so. There's nothing to forget. Good lord, woman, if I'd been interested in Jessica, I'd plenty of chances in the last year. Down at the beach that night I told her that I thought you were a stubborn fool and needed to be whipped into shape."

"Charming . . . "

"But that I intended to marry you. What happened after that was merely Jessica's way of 'parting friends.' Then, of course . . . the next morning I found that you'd already run off."

"I was so miserable—I couldn't help it. I didn't even want to see you again. Every time we were together, things got worse. I thought you couldn't stand the sight of me."

"It was my only defense. I didn't know a man could fall in love that fast," he admitted. "I certainly didn't plan to."

"Then you weren't thinking about vine-covered cottages when you invited me for that dinner date at the beach? That morning we met at Canfield?"

He grinned wryly. "Not that you'd notice. It wasn't your beautiful mind that attracted me at first. Not when you appeared in that scandalous outfit decorated with a shower fixture. I had to stand under a blast of cold water for five minutes afterwards before I could think straight. Then, of course, you had to show up here and display a whole list of assets I hadn't planned on. I knew I was going down for the count— it was only a matter of time."

"That's why you were so annoyed the day of our picnic?"

"Naturally." The laughter lines at the edge of his eyes deepened. "What man wants to be a weak-kneed invalid in the corner while his girl has to drive him home."

"Completely ignoring all the times you pulled *me* out of scrapes. And then when you came into the cave for me, I thought Les had killed you." She rubbed her forehead with trembling fingers. "I still can't bear to think about it."

"Then don't." Deke came across to take her coffee cup gently from her hand and put it on the bureau.

"We don't have to. I'm only sorry that Obie can't forget it, as well."

"He hasn't heard anything?"

Deke shook his head. "No bodies have been washed ashore near the accident. Personally, I think Les made it across the border. At any rate, he won't risk coming back to this neighborhood. Obie can have a job at the lodge as long as he wants. I thought we might keep the place as a base of operation." He paused and added with unfamiliar deference, "If that sounds all right to you. I know that this kind of life is different from what you're used to, darling, but I've thought about it a lot . . . "

"Not half as much as I have," she told him tremulously. "I don't care where I live as long as it's with you. I've been loving you so long that I still can't believe this is real."

"If I start to kiss you again, you'll know for sure." He held her at arm's length but his look embraced her. "It's too bad we only have a little while until that mail boat comes back."

"And then what happens?"

"We head for the courthouse at Gold Beach and I stake my claim."

"I must say it's taken you long enough," she teased.

"Camp follower!" He yanked at a strand of her hair, letting her know that he wasn't unaware of her motives. "I wanted to be sure of my ground. That I wasn't trespassing on somebody else's domain." There was a certain anxiety in his expression even then.

"You weren't." Melanie couldn't have been more

definite. "Absolutely a clear title to the territory." Her lips curved. "What about a claim marker? There must be some pink ribbon left . . ."

"We'll detour by the jeweler's and pick up something." His mouth brushed the soft skin at her temple. "Guaranteeing all the rights and privileges thereto," he said huskily.

Melanie's heartbeat thundered in her ears as her arms stole up around his neck. "For how long?" she whispered, wanting to draw out the enchanted moment.

He kept his voice solemn. "In a case like this, where it's agreeable to both parties, we usually suggest ninety-nine years as a nominal term."

"Ummm . . ." Her lips wandered in a whisper-light trail along his jaw. "That should do nicely. No problem there."

The touch of her soft body against his made Deke's resolutions vanish in a sudden surge of desire. "You're wrong there, my darling," he managed to say as he pulled her even closer. "I can tell you right now that ninety-nine years isn't going to be nearly long enough."

About the Author

Glenna Finley is a native of Washington State. She earned her degree from Stanford University in Russian Studies and in Speech and Dramatic Arts, with emphasis on radio.

After a stint in radio and publicity work in Seattle, she went to New York City to work for NBC as a producer in its international division. In addition, she worked with the "March of Time" and *Life* magazine.

As a producer, she had her own show about activities in Manhattan, a show that was broadcast to England. The programs were similar to those of the "Voice of America."

Though her life in New York was exciting, she eventually returned to the Northwest where she married. Currently residing in Seattle with her husband, Donald Witte, and their son, she loves to travel, and draws heavily on her travels and experiences for the novels that have been published. Her books for NAL have sold several million copies.

Have You Read These Big Bestsellers from SIGNET?

More Big Bestsellers from SIGNET

☐ **THE SAMURAI by George Macbeth.** (#J7021—$1.95)

☐ **FOR THE DEFENSE by F. Lee Bailey.** (#J7022—$1.95)

☐ **DRAGONS AT THE GATE by Robert Duncan.**
(#J6984—$1.95)

☐ **TREMOR VIOLET by David Lippincott.**
(#E6947—$1.75)

☐ **THE VOICE OF ARMAGEDDON by David Lippincott.**
(#W6412—$1.50)

☐ **YESTERDAY IS DEAD by Dallas Barnes.**
(#W6898—$1.50)

☐ **LOSERS, WEEPERS by Edwin Silberstang.**
(#W6798—$1.50)

☐ **THE PLASTIC MAN by David J. Gerrity.**
(#Y6950—$1.25)

☐ **THE BIRD IN LAST YEAR'S NEST by Shaun Herron.**
(#E6710—$1.75)

☐ **THE WHORE MOTHER by Shaun Herron.**
(#W5854—$1.50)

☐ **A GARDEN OF SAND by Earl Thompson.**
(#J6679—$1.95)

☐ **TATTOO by Earl Thompson.** (#E6671—$2.25)

☐ **FEAR OF FLYING by Erica Jong.** (#J6139—$1.95)

☐ **MISSION TO MALASPIGA by Evelyn Anthony.**
(#E6706—$1.75)

☐ **CLANDARA by Evelyn Anthony.** (#W6893—$1.50)

THE NEW AMERICAN LIBRARY, INC.,
P.O. Box 999, Bergenfield, New Jersey 07621

Please send me the SIGNET BOOKS I have checked above. I am
enclosing $_____(check or money order—no currency
or C.O.D.'s). Please include the list price plus 25¢ a copy to cover
handling and mailing costs. (Prices and numbers are subject to
change without notice.)

Name_____

Address_____

City_____State_____Zip Code_____
Allow at least 3 weeks for delivery

NAL/ABRAMS' BOOKS
ON ART, CRAFTS AND SPORTS
in beautiful large format, special
concise editions—lavishly illustrated
with many full-color plates.